"You've Never D0959237

Logan shook his head. "Nope."

Suddenly Cassie walked around the opposite end of the table and placed her daughter against his wide chest.

The baby squirmed, and Logan automatically shifted her to sit on his left forearm, while he splayed his right hand on her tiny back for support. He wasn't sure, but it must have been what she wanted, because she flashed him a grin. He couldn't help himself. He smiled right back. As far as babies went, Cassie's kids were the cutest he'd ever seen. And the one he held certainly seemed happy enough.

"For a man who's never been around babies, you're a natural. I bet you'll be a great father someday," Cassie said. "Babies sense whom they can trust and whom they can't. If Chelsea didn't trust you completely, she'd be fussing instead of snuggling against you."

Logan suddenly felt the need to run like hell. If Cassie thought she'd charm him into accepting the situation by having him hold a baby and flashing her killer dimples, she'd better think again.

What did he know about babies? Absolutely nothing. He most definitely *was not* father material. Not by a long shot. And that's just the way he intended it to stay. The way it had to stay...

Dear Reader,

Looking for romances with a healthy dose of passion? Don't miss Silhouette Desire's red-hot May lineup of passionate, powerful and provocative love stories!

Start with our MAN OF THE MONTH, *His Majesty, M.D.,* by bestselling author Leanne Banks. This latest title in the ROYAL DUMONTS miniseries features an explosive engagement of convenience between a reluctant royal and a determined heiress. Then, in Kate Little's *Plain Jane & Doctor Dad,* the new installment of Desire's continuity series DYNASTIES: THE CONNELLYS, a rugged Connelly sweeps a pregnant heroine off her feet.

A brooding cowboy learns about love and family in *Taming Blackhawk,* a SECRETS! title by Barbara McCauley. Reader favorite Sara Orwig offers a brand-new title in the exciting TEXAS CATTLEMAN'S CLUB: THE LAST BACHELOR series. In *The Playboy Meets His Match,* enemies become lovers and then some.

A sexy single mom is partnered with a lonesome rancher in Kathie DeNosky's *Cassie's Cowboy Daddy.* And in Anne Marie Winston's *Billionaire Bachelors: Garrett,* sparks fly when a tycoon shares a cabin with the woman he believes was his stepfather's mistress.

Bring passion into your life this month by indulging in all six of these sensual sizzlers.

Enjoy!

Joan Marlow Golan

Joan Marlow Golan
Senior Editor, Silhouette Desire

Please address questions and book requests to:
Silhouette Reader Service
U.S.: 3010 Walden Ave., P.O. Box 1325, Buffalo, NY 14269
Canadian: P.O. Box 609, Fort Erie, Ont. L2A 5X3

Cassie's Cowboy Daddy

KATHIE DeNOSKY

Published by Silhouette Books

America's Publisher of Contemporary Romance

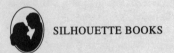 SILHOUETTE BOOKS

ISBN 0-373-76439-1

CASSIE'S COWBOY DADDY

This edition published by arrangement with Harlequin Books S.A.

® and TM are trademarks of Harlequin Books S.A., used under license.
Trademarks indicated with ® are registered in the United States Patent
and Trademark Office, the Canadian Trade Marks Office and in other
countries.

Visit Silhouette at www.eHarlequin.com

Printed in U.S.A.

Books by Kathie DeNosky

Silhouette Desire

Did You Say Married?! #1296
The Rough and Ready Rancher #1355
His Baby Surprise #1374
Maternally Yours #1418
Cassie's Cowboy Daddy #1439

KATHIE DeNOSKY

lives in deep southern Illinois with her husband and three children. After reading and enjoying Silhouette books for many years, she is ecstatic about being able to share her stories with others as a Silhouette Desire author, and writes highly sensual stories with a generous amount of humor. Kathie's books have appeared on the Waldenbooks bestseller list. She enjoys going to rodeos, traveling through the southern and southwestern states, and listening to country music. She often starts her day at 2:00 a.m., so she can write without interruption, before the rest of the family is up and about. You may write to Kathie at P.O. Box 2064, Herrin, Il 62948-5264.

Special thanks to Melissa Henke for sharing her knowledge and answering my endless questions about Wyoming and the Laramie Mountains. Thanks, Lissa!

One

Cassie Wellington explored the upper level of the large two-story Victorian, her enthusiasm increasing with each new discovery. The Lazy Ace ranch house was perfect, and all she'd ever dreamed of for herself and the girls.

The bedrooms were spacious, with beautifully detailed cherry woodwork, wainscoting and built-in window seats. But the most attractive thing about it was the fact that half of it belonged to her.

Everything from the molding on the ceiling to the hardwood floor needed a good dusting, and there was enough clutter downstairs to warrant the use of a shovel, but that could be excused. Her business partner was at least eighty years old and obviously no longer capable of simple household tasks. She'd whip this place into shape, and in no time she'd make a comfortable home for all of them. Then once everything had undergone a thorough cleaning, she'd start redecorating.

Preoccupied with ideas for window dressings, color combinations and where she intended to place each piece of furniture, she wandered into the hall bathroom and stumbled over something in the middle of the floor. She glanced down at a pile of boots, jeans and briefs at her feet, then to the long bare leg dangling over the side of the old-fashioned, claw-footed bathtub. The small space was filled to over-flowing with an impressively big, undeniably masculine body.

Her gaze followed the limb into the water.

Clear water.

She clapped her hand over her mouth to hold back her startled gasp and quickly averted her eyes to the safer territory of the man's torso.

Safer?

She'd never seen so many well-defined muscles on one body in her entire life. Covered by a thin coating of dark hair, his ridged stomach looked as hard as a rock and his corded shoulders seemed to span the entire width of the bathtub.

Her gaze traveled to his face and a shiver ran the length of her spine and made goose bumps pop up on her arms. Even in sleep, the man was dangerously handsome.

Thick black hair fell across his forehead much like that of a naughty little boy's, but the dark growth of beard shadowing his lean cheeks and the mustache framing his mouth were undoubtedly those of a man in his prime. The tiny lines fanning from the corners of his closed eyes attested to the fact that he spent the majority of his time working outside. Instead of detracting from his looks, they added a ruggedness to his overall appeal that Cassie found absolutely fascinating.

But when she looked more closely, her heart lurched, then started hammering at her vocal cords for an immediate response. Intense blue eyes gazed back at her from beneath thick black lashes.

"Go ahead and look your fill, sugar," the man offered. His sexy grin made her heart skip a beat. "I'm agreeable, even though we haven't been properly introduced."

"Oh, I'm so…I mean, you're…" Cassie clapped a hand over her mouth again to keep from making matters worse and started backing from the room.

"No need to leave, sugar." He pulled his leg back into the tub and sat up. His bluer-than-sin eyes twinkled and he had the audacity to wink at her. "You're just in time to help wash my back."

She took another step backward, but her foot came down on top of a boot. To her horror, she lost her balance and sat down hard on top of the pile of clothes.

"Are you all right?" the man asked, concern replacing his teasing grin. He braced his hands on the sides of the bathtub as if he intended to stand.

Cassie scrambled to her feet. In her haste to put as much distance as possible between herself and the man getting out of the tub, she stumbled over the other boot. This time she managed to stay upright, but just barely.

"Please don't get up. I'm fine. Really."

He laughed and shook his head. "Now, what kind of a gentleman would I be if I didn't stand when a lady enters the room? Just let me get out of here and…"

Logan saw it coming just as surely as a bubble rises to the surface of a boiling pot. But there wasn't a thing he could do to stop the pretty young woman from looking him square in the eyes and screaming bloody murder, before she spun around and ran for the stairs.

He'd been aware of her presence the moment she'd stepped into the room and, like any good poker player, he'd tried to size up the situation before showing his hand. But he couldn't think of one single reason this little filly would be wandering around his home. He laughed, realizing, in this particular situation, he'd been revealing a hell of a lot more than just his hand.

"Damn," he muttered when he tried to get out of the tub.

The stiff muscles in his back protested his every move and his leg had gone numb from hanging over the side of the tub. Every time he attempted to stand, he slid back into a sitting position. Ignoring the pins-and-needles sensation in his leg, he finally managed to get the limb to support him and splashed out of the water with a muttered curse.

Knotting a towel around his hips, Logan took off in the direction the woman had fled. He chuckled as he limped down the stairs. He hadn't meant to scare her, but he'd bet a steak dinner the little lady thought twice before she wandered into another house unannounced.

Of course, that wasn't to say he found her presence offensive. On the contrary. A man would have to be out of his mind to object to a woman like this one keeping him company while he took a bath. Shoot, he wouldn't even have minded having her join him.

Although she was shorter than the women he usually found attractive, she for damn sure had all the right curves in all the right places. And that strawberry-blond hair of hers made his hands itch to touch it, to pull off that puffy little pink thing holding it in a ponytail and see if it felt as soft and silky as it looked.

"What's your name, sugar?" he asked, catching up to her in the kitchen.

When she spun around to face him, a rosy pink colored her cheeks and anger sparkled in her green eyes. "It doesn't matter who *I* am. Who are *you?*"

Logan propped his hands on his hips, anchoring the towel in place. Smiling, he shook his head and took a step forward. "I asked first."

She held one hand in front of her as if that would stop him. He almost laughed. She sure had her share of spunk. He liked that in a woman.

"Stay right there," she ordered. "Don't you dare come any closer."

She tried to step away from him, but the cabinets stopped her retreat. Never taking her eyes from him, she put her hand behind her back and Logan heard her rummaging around in one of the drawers. Now, what in hell did she think she'd find in there?

"Don't take another step," she ordered, jerking her hand from behind her.

He frowned at her defensive stance and the pancake turner she brandished. He was in his own home and, even though she had to be the best-looking intruder he'd ever laid eyes on, she was still trespassing. And, he decided, staring at the flimsy utensil under his nose, a bit unstable.

"Look, lady, I don't know what your problem is or where you came from, but around these parts, barging in when a man's taking a bath could only be considered one of two things—an invasion of privacy or an open invitation."

He reached out to take her weapon, but let out a yelp when she used it like a flyswatter to smack him right square on his bare chest.

Logan quickly took hold of her upper arms before she had a chance to take aim at something a lot more sensitive than his chest. His gaze locking with hers, he drew her to him.

The pancake turner clattered to the hardwood floor. They both ignored it.

"You weren't supposed to do that," she said, her voice shaky and her expressive green eyes as wide as half dollars. "You were supposed to jump back so I could escape."

"But I didn't," Logan whispered close to her ear.

He heard her suck in a sharp breath a moment before she went perfectly still. Then with renewed vigor she started squirming like a worm on a hot sidewalk. "Turn me loose."

"Not until you calm down, sugar," Logan drawled. He stared down at her perfectly shaped lips. Lips just made for a man's kiss.

Lord help him, but she felt good pressed against him. She was small, delicate and soft. Really soft.

He inhaled deeply, and the sweet scent of her made his body feel as if his skin had suddenly grown way too tight. Where had he smelled that exotic scent before?

He didn't have long to ponder the matter because suddenly everything seemed to be happening at once. Her fidgeting caused the knot to come loose. Gravity pulled at his towel. And his foreman, Hank Waverly, and a tall blonde woman chose that very moment to come crashing through the back door.

Logan barely managed to maintain his hold on the woman and grab the towel before anyone's sensibilities were offended. "You'd better stand still. That was too close for comfort, sugar."

"Stop calling me that," she retorted. "And please let me go."

"Why on earth did you scr—" The blonde with Hank stopped short and stood there staring as if she'd never seen a man in danger of losing his towel.

The woman Logan held struggled to free herself. "Throw this exhibitionist off the property, Hank."

"Dammit, lady, if you don't stand still, there'll be an exhibition we'll all remember for some time to come," Logan growled.

"Oh, pul-lease," she said, rolling her eyes. "I wouldn't say your attributes are *that* memorable."

She increased her attempts to free herself, sending pain shooting through his knotted muscles as he struggled to hold her and the towel. His curses could have blistered paint, but he didn't care.

For a minute there, when he'd gazed into her sparkling eyes and felt her soft body pressed to his, he'd forgotten all about his sore back. And he'd come damned close to kissing her, he thought incredulously, trying his best to hold both the woman and the towel.

Taking advantage of his predicament, she jerked free and stepped well out of his reach. He caught the terry cloth just in time to keep it from exposing his nether regions.

"Does Logan Murdock know you use his bathtub when he's away?" she demanded.

Hank threw back his head and laughed like a hyena. "Oh, this is good. Real good."

Logan barely suppressed his own grin. He'd been wrong. She wasn't "a bit unstable." She was downright loco. Securing the towel before it revealed more than he cared to show, he raised a brow. "You and Murdock close, are you?"

"Close enough," she replied.

"Do tell." It took everything he had to keep a straight face at her confident expression. She really was a few steers shy of a full herd.

"From now on, you can bathe in the bunkhouse with the rest of the men." She pointed toward the hall. "Now, get your clothes and get out of my house."

"Your house!" All traces of amusement gone, Logan shot a suspicious glare at Hank when the man doubled over and slapped his knee. "Just where the hell did you come up with a harebrained idea like that?"

"My lawyer."

Apprehension plucked at the hair on the back of his neck and he narrowed his eyes. "Just who are you, lady?"

"Not that it's any of your business, but I'm Logan Murdock's business partner, Cassie Wellington. I own half of the Lazy Ace."

"You're the Widow Wellington?" Logan shook his head. He wasn't buying a word of it. "You can come up with a better story than that, sugar."

Barely able to speak, Hank said cheerfully, "Welcome home, Logan."

A keening wail suddenly sliced through the tense silence. A second cry soon joined in.

Goose bumps rose along Logan's arms and a tight knot formed in the pit of his belly. "What the hell is that?" he demanded, afraid he already knew.

Cassie's world came to a screeching halt. Logan? Hank had called the man Logan.

Studying him, she felt the color drain from her face. His black hair didn't have so much as one strand of white, and the only wrinkles he had were the tiny ones at the corners of his deep blue eyes.

Instead of the frail, elderly gentleman she had envisioned, Logan Murdock was drop-dead handsome and only a few years older than herself. Her gaze traveled to his wide bare chest. His physique for darned sure wasn't that of a man in his golden years, either.

No bags. No sags. Just warm, incredibly firm muscle.

Remembering the feel of being pressed against all that hard sinew made her cheeks burn and toes curl inside her tennis shoes. "Logan? Murdock?"

"In the flesh," Hank said, dissolving into another fit of laughter.

Cassie's best friend, Ginny Sadler, stepped from

behind Hank to stare at the man claiming to be Logan Murdock. "Oh, dear heavens! I thought you said he was as old as your uncle Silas."

"You can't possibly be Mr. Murdock," Cassie insisted, hoping this was some sort of joke. "He's away from the ranch and I happen to know he's elderly."

"Well, you couldn't possibly be the Widow Wellington," he said. The man's gaze traveled in a leisurely way from the top of her head to her well-worn shoes. "You don't look old enough to be married, let alone widowed." Frowning at the continued wails of her unhappy daughters, he asked, "Is that yours?"

"Yes." Cassie turned to Ginny. "Would you mind checking on the twins for me?"

His disbelieving gaze zeroed in on her waist. "If you've had twins, I'm the king of Siam."

"Aren't you a little far from home, *Your Highness?*" When a dull red flush made its way from his neck to the roots of his hair, she smiled, satisfied that the "king" was as royally disconcerted by the whole situation as she was.

Hank laughed so hard he had to lean against the cabinets. "This is better than the time we greased down Gabe's saddle with axle grease and watched him go shootin' off the other side when he tried to mount up."

Eyeing his foreman, Logan breathed a heavy sigh and began to chuckle. "I have to admit, you really outdid yourself this time, Hank. You really had me going there for a minute."

Hank glanced at Cassie, her obvious displeasure

erasing all traces of his amusement. Logan felt the knot in his gut tighten considerably.

"Uh...Logan, she *is* Cassie Wellington, your new business partner."

Logan's smile vanished, but he refused to give up hope. "You've had your fun, but the game's over." He pointed to the woman calling herself the Widow Wellington. "As soon as they're ready, drive all of them down to Bear Creek. They can play jokes on someone else."

She shook her head. "This is no joke. And I'm not going anywhere."

"My partner's name is Cassandra." He knew as soon as he blurted out the irrational statement he was grasping at straws. But desperation was beginning to claw at him.

"Everyone calls me Cassie. My full name is Cassandra Hastings-Wellington."

Logan felt his control of the situation take a nose-dive, and that sinking feeling that always accompanied a lost cause began to settle in his gut. The Widow Wellington wasn't at all what he'd expected when he first heard about Silas Hastings's death and the naming of the man's heir.

She was supposed to be a widow, for Pete's sake. Logan had naturally envisioned a matronly, grandmother type with a big heart and a girth to match.

But the woman's light pink T-shirt, tucked into snug-fitting jeans, emphasized a waist he could wrap his hands all the way around. And the enticing flare of her slim hips was light-years away from matronly. He had a hard time believing she'd had one baby, let alone a set of twins.

The stranglehold he had on the towel made his fingers cramp. He'd judge her to be somewhere in her mid-twenties and much too pretty for his peace of mind. Those green eyes of hers were the color of new spring grass—all fresh and sweet. And her creamy complexion just begged for his touch.

His palm started itching to do just that. He rubbed his hand against the plush towel in an effort to make the sensation go away.

There were two kinds of women—free spirits and nesters. A free spirit lived for the moment and demanded no more of a man than he was ready—or willing—to give. And that was just the type of woman Logan preferred.

But a nester was an entirely different breed. They wanted stability and long-range promises. They wanted a home that wasn't to hell and gone from civilization and all the conveniences that went with it. Unfortunately, his new business partner had nester written from the top of her pretty little head all the way to her tattered tennis shoes.

Sweat beaded Logan's forehead. The Widow Wellington represented a little over five feet of sexy temptation he'd rather not have around testing his willpower. Or reminding him of what he had to deny himself for the Lazy Ace.

He'd learned the hard way that the land was just too harsh for the fairer sex. Too remote. After making a fool of himself ten years ago, he'd successfully avoided Cassie Wellington's kind and the commitments they put such stock in. And come hell or high water, that's just the way he wanted it to remain— the way it *had* to remain.

"I don't give a damn what you say, lady. You *will* be leaving as soon as possible."

She propped her doubled fists on her shapely little hips. The action once again drew his attention to the narrowness of her waist, the fullness of her breasts. He almost groaned.

"I'm not going anywhere," she said stubbornly. "My daughters and I will stay as long as we darn well please. My uncle's will plainly stated that I own half of this ranch *and* half of the ranch house. It's as much mine as it is yours, buster."

"Like hell!" His stiff back forgotten, Logan spun around and once again had to grab the towel as he headed for his office. But when he reached the hall, he stopped abruptly and turned to glare at Hank. "If you can tear yourself away, I'd like to see you in the study. You owe me some answers. And they'd better be damned good."

Cassie stared at Logan's retreating back a moment before she leveled her own irritated gaze on Hank. "When I called last week to inquire about moving here, you said Mr. Murdock had been alone for so many years that our presence would be good for him, that we were just what he needed to give him a new lease on life. That and the photo I have led me to believe he was an older gentleman. Why didn't you tell me he was younger than Uncle Silas?"

Hank's smile faded and he shifted from one foot to the other. "I'm...uh, real sorry if you feel I misled you, ma'am. I sure didn't mean to. I just figured you knew he was a lot younger than your uncle."

Cassie shook her head and walked over to the cabinet where she'd set her handbag when she'd first entered the house. Searching inside the leather tote, she pulled out a picture of two men standing under the Lazy Ace Cattle Company sign that hung over the entrance to the ranch. She handed it to Hank. "Read the caption on the back."

"Logan Murdock and Silas Hastings. Joint owners. Fall 1954." Hank nodded. "This explains the confusion. Logan was named after his grandpa. That's him in the picture with your uncle. They were both in their early thirties when it was taken."

Cassie tried to swallow the panic threatening to break through. Logan Murdock wasn't the kind, elderly gentleman she'd envisioned. He'd turned out to be a ruggedly handsome, thirty-something hunk with an attitude.

Ginny returned from checking on the twins, her eyes wide. "What on earth are you going to do now, Cassie? You and the girls can't possibly stay here."

Dazed, Cassie looked around the room. The house was perfect for raising children and so much nicer than the cramped apartment they'd left behind in St. Louis. It was everything she'd ever dreamed of for the twins.

She straightened her shoulders. She'd fought one man for their very existence. She wasn't afraid to fight another for their future.

"Come on, Ginny," she said, walking to the door. "We need to unload the car."

Her friend hurried to keep up with her. "You can't mean—"

"Yes, I can," Cassie said, determination filling her soul.

"He's not going to like it," Ginny warned.

"That's his problem." Cassie stepped out onto the porch and watched an eagle flying high above the valley. "I'm not letting some arrogant cowboy deprive my daughters of what's rightfully theirs. We're staying, and Logan Murdock will just have to learn to live with it."

Two

"**D**ammit all, Hank!" Logan glared at the man closing the office door. "How the hell did this happen?"

Hank calmly walked over and sat down in the leather chair in front of Logan's desk. "Not more than half an hour after you took off for that campin' trip last Friday, she called to say she and her babies would be movin' here."

Unable to sit still, Logan rose from the desk chair and stalked over to the huge picture window. Pride filled him as he surveyed *his* land. Bathed by the early-autumn sun, the dried grass spread out like a golden carpet and the aspens ringing the valley shuddered from the winds of the changing season. He watched a bald eagle trace lazy circles in the cloudless blue sky. Dammit, this land belonged to *him*.

"You didn't even try to discourage her, did you?"

"Nope," Hank said, sounding unrepentant.

Logan felt a vein in his temple begin to throb as he glared over his shoulder. "Why not?"

Hank stared at his boot tops, then, shrugging, met Logan's gaze. "She sounded so happy about it, I couldn't tell her not to move here."

"She's happy, all right." His hands propped on his hips, Logan turned to face his friend. "Happy to get her hands on *my* ranch."

"It's as much hers as it is yours."

Logan winced as his sore muscles tightened further. "I didn't see any of the Hastings family anywhere near here when the temperature dipped down to twenty below last winter and we had to chop holes in the ice for the cattle to get water." He pointed toward the window. "Or two years ago, when lightning touched off the fire that swept down the mountains into the valley. There wasn't one of them here busting their asses to help us save the house and barns."

"I know," Hank agreed. "But, legally, she is an equal partner in the Lazy Ace."

"I don't give a damn about legalities," Logan said through gritted teeth. He ran his hand over the aching knot at the back of his neck.

Hank had no way of knowing Logan's plan, or that if Logan was successful in his bid to obtain all of the ranch, then Hank would gain an interest in the enterprise. Logan owed it to him for the loyalty and years of hard work Hank had invested in the Lazy Ace. But if Logan couldn't get Cassie Wellington to sell him her share, all his carefully laid plans would go to hell in a handbasket.

"I have to figure a way to get her to sell out and leave," he muttered.

"I like havin' ladies and babies around," Hank said happily. "It dresses up this old place right nice."

Glaring at his lifelong friend, Logan tightened the towel at his waist. "You know, old buddy, the only thing softer than your heart is your head."

"I can't help it," Hank said. The man's wide grin irritated the hell out of Logan. "When it comes to women and cute little kids—"

"Your common sense takes a hike." Logan marched back to his chair and plopped down. Propping his elbows on the desktop, he buried his head in his hands. "What the hell could old Silas have been thinking when he left his share of the ranch to a woman? He knew how remote this place is. And how dangerous it can be at times."

"Maybe the old codger wanted the two families to merge," Hank suggested.

Logan jerked his head up. "Before that happens, Murray Parkinson's jackass will sprout wings and fly. You know how I feel about having a woman underfoot all the time."

"Especially one as pretty as Cassie?"

Logan ground his teeth, then lied right through them. "She's not *that* good-looking."

"Uh-huh."

"She's not," Logan insisted.

"If you say so," Hank said, looking like the cat that swallowed the canary.

Before Logan could decide whether to defend himself further or just give up and choke Hank, a soft female voice outside the closed door announced, "Gentlemen, dinner's ready."

Surprised, Logan and Hank looked at each other, then at the closed door.

"Are you sure you don't want her stickin' around?" Hank asked, jumping to his feet. "We ain't had a decent meal around this place in a month of Sundays."

"Don't let Tucker hear you say that," Logan said, heading for the door. "He might just up and quit."

"I don't care if he does." Hank shouldered past Logan to bolt out the door into the hall. "Ol' Tuck used to be pretty fair as bunkhouse cooks go. But since he got too vain to buy himself a pair of glasses, we've been eatin' stuff a starvin' dog would turn down."

Logan nodded and started toward the stairs. "The other day I caught him trying to make a cake from a feed-store receipt. I had the devil's own time trying to convince him it wasn't a recipe."

While Hank headed for the kitchen like a man possessed, Logan took the stairs two at a time. After quickly exchanging the towel for jeans and a chambray shirt, he entered the kitchen a few minutes later.

Stopping abruptly, he barely managed to keep from gaping at the unfamiliar sight. It looked like an all-out female invasion. Bright clothing added splashes of color to the normally somber room as the Widow Wellington and her friend milled around his table and fussed over the girl babies riding their hips. Feminine voices replaced the usual silence and Logan was more than a little irritated that he found the sound a pleasant variation.

He shook his head when he watched Hank set up two high chairs. The man looked disgustingly happy.

Hank glanced up and grinned as he set the chairs at the end of the table. "It sure was nice of these ladies to fix our supper after bein' on the road for the last two days. Wasn't it, Logan?"

All eyes turned to solemnly stare at him. Even the copper-haired babies.

When he walked to the head of the large oak table, the widow set a plate of sandwiches on the recently polished surface. "Mr. Murdock, this is my friend, Ginny Sadler. She'll be staying with us for a few days." The look she gave him clearly challenged any objections he might have. Then she pointed to the identical babies, adding, "And these are my daughters, Kelsie and Chelsea."

The blonde she'd called Ginny smiled weakly and edged her way toward Hank.

Logan nodded his acknowledgment, but his grim stare remained fixed on the widow and the domestic picture laid out before him. She looked at home in his kitchen, and she'd apparently already started nesting. He wouldn't have believed the old table could shine up that nicely.

He flicked a frilly piece of cloth from his spot at the table, sending it skittering across the shiny surface. "Where the devil did that come from?"

"I brought it with me," she replied, returning the offending object to its place. "Don't tell me you've never seen a linen napkin."

"Not on my table," Logan growled. He seated

himself, then once again pushed the cloth aside. "You're on a working ranch in the middle of Wyoming, lady, not some fancy restaurant."

"I'm well aware of that," she said calmly.

He watched her place the babies in their chairs. Then in one smooth motion she replaced his napkin and plopped a set of silverware on top of it, as if that ended any further protest he might have.

Logan knew he was being unreasonable, but with each passing second he could feel his blissful bachelor existence slipping further away. He wasn't accustomed to having females, and especially one with babies, in his home. And the Widow Wellington appeared to be one of the worst of her gender.

He could tell by just looking at her that she'd make demands and all kinds of things would change. For as long as she and her brood stayed on the Lazy Ace, she'd expect him to watch his language when a graphic, heartfelt cussing would feel good—help him put things in perspective. And he for damned sure wouldn't be able to sit around in his underwear and watch television anymore, either. Not that he practiced that particular habit all that often, but just knowing he couldn't had him lamenting the loss.

Good thing the master bedroom had a half bath. At least he wouldn't have her glaring daggers at him when he left the toilet seat up.

Frowning, Logan took a bite from his sandwich and watched the women laugh at something Hank said. Unlike his friend, Logan had no intention of letting some woman lead him around like a puppy on a string. He'd seen that happen to some of his neighbors in the Rancher's Emporium down in Bear

Creek. While their women tried on clothes in the dressing rooms, the men stood around holding prissy little handbags in their big brawny fists, discussing the advantages of artificial insemination over a good breeding bull. The big galoots didn't even have enough sense to look as if they found the experience humiliating.

"Logan?" Hank waved his hand in front of Logan's face. "I asked if you found any signs of the cougar Ray reported seeing up in the high pastures while you were on your camping trip."

Snapped out of his dismal speculation, Logan shook his head and swallowed what tasted like sawdust slapped between two slices of bread. "I tracked him all over the northwestern quadrant, but never did catch sight of him. When I reached the waterfall at the end of Shadow Valley, the tracks disappeared."

"Do you have a lot of trouble with wild animals?" Cassie inquired.

He watched her spoon some of the nastiest-looking green stuff he'd ever seen from small jars and into the babies' eager mouths. It looked as if their supper wasn't any more palatable than his. So much for the widow's cooking.

"Well, do you?"

"Huh?"

"I asked if you have a lot of trouble with wild animals."

He studied her curious expression. Maybe if he mentioned a wild animal or two, she'd decide it was far too dangerous for her and her kids and take off like a coyote with a buttful of buckshot.

"Sometimes," Logan said slowly.

"Oh, speaking of wild animals, Samson paid us a visit while you were gone," Hank said, as if on cue.

"Who or what is Samson?" Ginny asked.

"One of the biggest black bears you'd ever care to see," Hank answered, leaning back in his chair.

Logan couldn't have been more pleased with the turn of conversation. Knowing Hank and his aversion to the bear Logan had raised from an orphaned cub, Samson would no doubt grow at least two feet in height and gain a couple of hundred pounds by the time Hank finished describing him.

"When that bear stands on his hind feet, he's every bit as big as a grizzly," Hank said.

Logan took another bite of his sandwich to keep from grinning. He couldn't have asked Hank for a better job of exaggerating the bear's size.

"Do you think he'll be back any time soon?" Cassie asked, continuing to spoon the unappealing mush from the jars and into the little girls' mouths.

"It wouldn't surprise me." When Ginny scooted her chair a little closer to his, a pleased expression lit Hank's face. "Old Samson has been known to hang around for days before he heads back up into the mountains."

A sense of contentment surrounded Logan. The widow and her entourage would be off the ranch, out of his life and headed back to St. Louis first thing in the morning.

Unable to resist adding a little fuel to the fire Hank had kindled, Logan tried to keep his tone pragmatic. "Wild animals are just one of the hazards of living in this part of the country. At times, the weather can be more dangerous than the wildlife."

"You might as well give it up, Mr. Murdock," Cassie said, setting the baby-food jar on the table. The clatter of the spoon inside the empty glass echoed throughout the suddenly quiet room. She knew what he was up to and the sooner he realized it wasn't going to work, the better off they'd both be. "You're not going to scare me away from what's rightfully mine. Whether you like it or not, the twins and I are here to stay."

The shroud of stillness that descended on the kitchen was deafening as she and Logan glared at each other across the big oak table. It reminded her of the unnatural calm before a huge storm.

"Hank, why don't you help me with the twins?" Ginny asked, finally breaking the tense silence. She rose from the table and began unfastening the safety straps on the high chairs. "I think these two need to talk."

"But it's just startin' to get interestin'," Hank protested. When Ginny leaned down to whisper something in his ear, Hank's face brightened and he left the table so fast his chair tilted precariously. "You're right. They don't need us. It's a fairly warm evening. Why don't we take the babies for a walk?"

Hank took Kelsie, while Ginny removed Chelsea from her high chair. "We're going to show the babies Velvet Lady's new colt." He waited for Ginny to wipe the twins' faces, then helped her wrestle matching yellow sweaters on them. They each held a baby as Hank ushered Ginny toward the door. "You two take all the time you need."

At any other time, Cassie might have found Hank's haste to be with Ginny quite comical. But considering that their departure left her alone with Logan, Cassie didn't see anything funny about it.

The man was raw virility personified, and from the moment he'd walked into the kitchen, every one of her senses had homed in on him like some type of feminine radar. The lingering scent of his masculine soap, the sight of his corded forearms beneath his rolled-up shirtsleeves and the sound of his slightly rough baritone had her remembering the feel of his callused hands on her upper arms. The memory of his nude body in the bathtub sent a shiver snaking up her spine that had nothing to do with being chilled.

"Ginny's right," Cassie said, her tone sharpened by the sudden tension gripping her body. "We need to discuss the terms of our partnership."

The harsh sound of Logan's chair scraping along the hardwood floor echoed through the room. "I couldn't agree more. There are some things we need to resolve, Mrs. Wellington. And I'd say now is as good a time as any to get it done."

"Since my children and I are going to be living here, don't you think it would be a good idea if we were on a first-name basis?" she asked, rising to face him.

He stared at her a moment before he nodded, stepped aside and motioned toward the hall. "All right, *Cassie*. Let's go into my study."

She normally hated confrontations, but she looked forward to this one. Logan Murdock needed to be treated to a few home truths. And the sooner, the better. She'd been around one too many selfish, self-centered men to let this one get the best of her.

She only wished his deep baritone hadn't sounded so sexy, or that she hadn't preceded him down the hall. His voice had that rough bedroom quality that sent a tremor passing through her when he said her name, and she could feel his gaze on her backside as surely as if he touched her there.

The man was, without a doubt, the most infuriating, obstinate soul Cassie had ever met. But he made her knees wobble and her lungs forget to take in air.

Logan brushed past her to open the door, and a tingle raced the length of her. Reminding herself to breathe, she entered the study and looked around in an attempt to distract herself from the unsettling reaction. To her disappointment, it was no different than any of the other rooms in the house—cherry wainscoting, massive pieces of leather-and-walnut furniture and neutral, nondescript drapes. It appeared Logan Murdock was stuck in a decorating rut.

"Does it meet with your approval?" he asked from somewhere behind her.

Cassie turned toward the sound of his voice, but instead of the snappy comeback she'd intended, she let loose a startled squeak. A huge bear in the corner loomed over Logan, mouth agape, claws extended, and after all the talk about Samson, it took a moment for her to realize the beast was poised for all eternity in the ferocious, battle-ready stance.

She shuddered and turned away. Instead of her gaze settling on something innocuous, she came face-to-face with the largest snake she'd ever seen outside the confines of a zoo. It was sitting in the middle of the mantel above the fireplace, four inches of rattles protruding from the tan-and-brown-blotched coil, the raised head promising a deadly bite from its enormous, bared fangs.

What sort of man kept such hideous works of taxidermy in his home? she wondered, spotting a lynx on the shelves beside the fireplace. The animal was frozen forever in what looked to be a really lousy mood.

"No wonder you keep this door closed," Cassie said, her voice slightly shaky. "No one in their right mind would want to come in here."

It was all Logan could do to keep from laughing out loud at Cassie's shocked expression. Her face had paled to a pasty white and she looked ready to bolt for the door. She had no way of knowing this room had scared the hell out of him when he was a kid. Or that the stuffed animals were a lot older than he was.

"They threatened the welfare of the Lazy Ace," he stated, lowering himself into the chair behind the desk. "When they attacked the livestock, my family had no choice but to deal with them."

"You see me as a threat." Cassie turned to glare at him. "Is this your way of telling me I'm the next to be stuffed and mounted?"

Logan watched her cheeks color a pretty pink as the double meaning of her words registered with both of them. He swallowed hard and his body responded in ways he'd rather not dwell on as a very provocative scenario flashed through his mind. This wasn't going the way he'd planned. He was supposed to be discussing her departure from the Lazy Ace, not trying to hide the fact that her remark excited the hell out of him.

"I...uh, never said you were a threat."

"You didn't have to." She sat in the leather chair in front of his desk, her arms crossed beneath her breasts, her expression defiant. "Once you found out who I was, you turned off the charm and turned on the hostility."

"You weren't exactly Miss Congeniality yourself." He leaned back in the high-backed chair and sighed heavily. "Look, taking potshots at each other isn't going to get us anywhere. What do you say we start over?"

"That sounds like a good idea," she agreed. "I think that might make our living here more tolerable."

Every time she mentioned staying on the ranch, the hair on the back of his neck stood straight up and his gut felt as if he'd been punched.

Logan squared his shoulders. He knew beyond a shadow of doubt he wasn't going to like what she had to say, but he'd always been of the opinion that a situation should be dealt with head-on.

"Why don't you tell me why you want to live here, then we'll go from there," he suggested.

"All right." She took a deep breath, then met his gaze. "Uncle Silas bequeathed money to my cousins, but his last wish for me and the twins was a new way of life. By leaving me his half of the Lazy Ace Cattle Company, he's provided me the opportunity to stay at home to raise my girls." Her relieved smile made the knot in Logan's gut twist even tighter. "I remember hearing Uncle Silas repeatedly say the unhurried pace of rural Wyoming was the perfect place to raise children. And he was right. It's much safer here, the girls will have a healthy atmosphere away from the smog and fumes of an overcrowded city, and I'll be with them to watch and enjoy every moment of their lives, instead of hearing about it from a baby-sitter.''

By the time she finished telling him about her desire to be a full-time mother and how important it was for her to raise her kids in a safe, wholesome environment, Logan felt as if he'd been blindsided by a steamroller. If he insisted she leave now, he'd feel like a low-down, sorry excuse for a skunk.

''Wouldn't you rather live in town?'' he asked hopefully. He knew all too well the dangers the area posed to women and children. But if he tried to explain that to her now, she'd think it was nothing more than a ploy to get her off the Lazy Ace.

She shook her head. ''I've analyzed it from every angle and arrived at the same conclusion each time. It was the nicest thing Uncle Silas could have ever done for us. I want the girls to grow up here where they can run and play.'' She gave him a pointed look. ''And I want to be here to oversee my share of the ranch.''

Logan left his chair to pace back and forth behind the desk. ''I could keep you informed of all business transactions in a quarterly report when I send a check for your part of the profits. Like I did for Silas.''

''Nothing against you, Mr. Murdock, but it's my inheritance and I think it would be in my best interest to be here in order to watch over it.''

''The Murdock and Hastings families have been in business together for over a hundred years….''

''I know,'' she said, nodding. ''I've heard the

story since I was old enough to listen—first from my father and grandfather, then after they passed away, from Uncle Silas. Your great-grandfather, Jake Murdock, and my great-grandfather, Ned Hastings, left St. Louis with nothing but their six-shooters and a deed for a large piece of prime ranch land they'd won in a poker game.''

"That's right," Logan agreed. "And it was your great-grandfather who lost interest and moved back to Missouri thirty-five years later," he said pointedly. "He and the rest of your family have been perfectly happy as silent partners in the ranch. The Murdocks were the ones who stuck it out and made the Lazy Ace what it is today."

"I'm well aware of that," she said, her patience beginning to wear on his nerves. "But when Uncle Silas willed me his share of the ranch, I made a firm decision to become an *active* partner. It's not fair that you and your family suffered all the hardships, while my family sat back and did nothing. Besides, I want to have firsthand knowledge of how you're handling our livelihood."

Logan stopped to glare at her. "I'm a man of my word. If that was good enough for your uncle, it should be good enough for you."

"I'm not my uncle, Mr. Murdock. Put yourself in my shoes. Would you trust someone you didn't know with the stakes this high?" When he remained silent, she smiled and rose to leave. "I'm no different. This is my children's future we're discussing and I'm not about to leave anything to chance."

"But what about your family?" Logan asked desperately. "Won't you miss seeing them?"

She shook her head. "There's no reason for me to ever return to St. Louis. My parents are both deceased and I don't have any brothers or sisters." Opening the office door, she advised, "You might as well accept the fact that, from now on, my daughters and I will be calling the Lazy Ace home."

He watched her close the door with a quiet click. "Not if I have anything to do with it, lady," he muttered.

Three

Cassie stood at the foot of the stairs, feather duster in one hand and a bottle of furniture polish in the other. Where should she start?

Yesterday, after finding Logan in the bathtub, she hadn't given cleaning the house a second thought. A warm shiver coursed through her. She doubted there was a woman alive who could think of dusting and polishing woodwork after seeing Logan Murdock in the buff.

And she'd told a real whopper yesterday when she'd said his body was unremarkable. Just the memory of all that masculine skin and the feel of those rock-hard muscles pressed against her had kept her awake most of the night. Which was about the dumbest thing she'd ever let happen. She wasn't the least bit interested in Logan or his impressive muscle groups.

Shaking her head to dislodge the memory of his impressive assets from her traitorous brain, she stared at the living room. The man might have a gorgeous body, but he was a slob. Plain and simple. And the reality of the monumental task before her was almost enough to make her rethink her decision to move to the Lazy Ace.

That's probably why he's not married. Any woman in her right mind would take one look at the condition of the house and run as hard and fast as she could to get away.

A saddle draped the back of one armchair, while an odd assortment of jeans, shirts and white cotton briefs graced the back of the other. Newspapers, magazines, cups and glasses covered the tables beside the chairs and the coffee table in front of the big leather couch.

Dazed, Cassie turned her attention to the stone fireplace on the far side of the room. The moose head hanging above the mantel sported a Colorado Rockies ball cap, a pair of oversize sunglasses and a necktie screen printed with popular cartoon characters.

"You've got to be kidding," Ginny said, walking up beside her. "It looks like a war zone."

Cassie nodded as she walked over to the fireplace to run the feather duster over the mantel. The cloud raised by the simple action made her sneeze. "When I called last week, Hank said the place needed a woman's touch." She picked up a pair of stiff socks from the stone hearth and held them at arm's length. "But he failed to mention I'd need a bulldozer to clear out the clutter. It's going to take me weeks to get this place into shape."

"Funny you should mention that," Ginny said, grinning. "Hank and I were talking just this morning about how much you'll have to do to get things straightened up."

"Tell me about it," Cassie said dryly. She sneezed again. "This place has dust bunnies the size of buffalo."

Ginny nodded. "And you're going to need help. If you don't mind putting up with me for another week or two, I think I'll call the office and ask for more time off."

"Oh, Ginny, I hate for you to use your vacation helping me clean." Cassie took the cap, tie and sunglasses from the moose's head. "But I'm not going to turn you down if you really want to stay."

"Good." Ginny's grin was a little too bright, considering the task before them. "I'll go find Hank and ask him if he'd mind moving some of this heavy furniture so we can clean under it."

Ginny couldn't hide the color in her cheeks or the sparkle in her eyes that had nothing whatsoever to do with thoughts of cleaning. It did, however, have everything to do with finding Hank.

Cassie truly felt sorry for her best friend. An incurable romantic, Ginny still believed in finding her knight in shining armor and living happily-ever-after.

But thanks to her late husband, Stan, that was a myth Cassie had abandoned a long time ago.

A knot of disappointment formed in her stomach at the thought of the man she'd vowed to cherish until death. When they married, Cassie had taken for granted that Stan would settle down and work with her to build a future. Unfortunately, that hadn't been the case.

They'd been married only a few months when Cassie realized that it had been Stan's self-centeredness, not immaturity, that prevented him from accepting the responsibilities of marriage. Even if he hadn't died, they wouldn't have stayed together.

She blinked back tears and shook her head. No, happily-ever-afters happened only in fairy tales.

Cussing a blue streak, Logan pitched a bale of straw over the side of the loft. Four more followed in rapid succession. When each one burst open from colliding with the dirt floor below, he gritted his teeth and barely suppressed the urge to growl. Instead of lessening the frustration burning in his gut, he'd only created more.

"Logan, you're bein' a real pain in the ass. I wish you'd get off your high horse." Hank propped his fists on his hips and nodded at the broken bales at his feet. "Now I'm gonna have to get the wheelbarrow so I can get this bedding down to Nicoma's stall."

"Maybe it'll keep you busy enough to avoid making a fool of yourself over the blonde," Logan shot back.

"Somebody in this barn is makin' a fool of himself, all right. But it ain't me." Hank laughed. "At least I've got the good sense to admit the scenery around this old place has improved a hell of a lot since yesterday."

Logan gripped the ladder and started down. "But for how long?"

He knew he was being irrational. But after tossing and turning all night from the memory of Cassie's soft body pressed against his, being reasonable wasn't an option.

Skipping the last two rungs, he jumped to the ground and jerked his thumb over his shoulder at the open doorway. "Just how long do you think it'll take before the boredom sets in with those two?"

"Maybe it won't. Not all females are like Andrea." Hank shook his head. "I never could see the two of you together. I doubt she would survive living anywhere that didn't include a mall and a four-star restaurant."

Snorting, Logan ignored the man's comment about his lapse in judgment. He didn't intend to waste time thinking about the past. It was Cassie Wellington and the present that bothered him. A lot.

"Once the widow and her friend figure out just how remote this place is, they won't be able to get away from here fast enough," Logan said, marching to the end of the barn. He grasped the wooden handles of the wheelbarrow and rolled it next to the broken bales of straw. "Just think how they'd react when winter hits and we're all snowed in for days at a time."

"That's when it starts to get interestin'," Hank said, his grin wide.

The thought of himself and Cassie stranded for several days, alone in the house with all those bedrooms to choose from, made Logan's mouth go dry.

Disgusted with himself for giving the notion a second thought, he spoke as much for his own benefit as for Hank's. "Stop thinking with your hormones and start thinking with your head. I doubt either one of them could make it to the first frost without going stir-crazy.''

"Then what are you worried about?'' Hank asked. He grabbed a pitchfork leaning against the wall and forked straw into the cart. "If what you say is true, Cassie and the babies should be packed up and on their way back to St. Louis by the last of the month.''

Logan shook his head and guided the wheelbarrow to the end of the barn. "It's not that easy.'' Stopping at the open stall, he turned to face Hank. "I always thought Silas was a few cards shy of a full deck, but I never realized the old codger had a mean streak to go with it. He knew about my mother dying because we couldn't get her to the hospital in time and the hell that broke loose afterward. But before he died, he filled Cassie's head with the idea that this place is some kind of Shangri-la for raising kids.''

"Well, it's where I intend to raise my kids,'' Hank said, shrugging.

"Hank?''

Logan watched Hank's face split into a wide grin at the sight of Ginny walking down the center aisle of the barn.

"And here comes the mother of those future kids,'' Hank said, his voice low.

"You just met the woman,'' Logan muttered.

"Doesn't matter.'' Hank handed him the pitchfork and headed toward Ginny. "I know what I want.''

Logan stared as Hank met Ginny halfway up the long corridor, took her into his arms and kissed her like a soldier returning from war. An image of Cassie in *his* arms, clinging to *him* as he kissed her, flashed through Logan's mind, and an unfamiliar feeling twisted his gut.

When Hank finally let her up for air, Ginny sounded breathless. "Cassie…and I…have been… cleaning the living room. Would you…mind helping us move some of the furniture?"

"Not at all." Hank tucked Ginny to his side and, staring down at her, added, "I'd be more than happy to help you do anything, honey." He kissed her forehead. "All you have to do is ask."

Logan felt the knot in his stomach tighten further when Ginny giggled and wrapped her arm around Hank's waist. Following the enamored pair into the house to see what the two women had done to his home, Logan refused to acknowledge the sensation as anything other than hunger. It was getting close to lunchtime and he'd skipped breakfast.

Envy for the freedom Hank had to give his heart to a woman was an emotion Logan didn't feel. Ever.

Cassie watched the men pick up the massive couch as if it weighed nothing and move it to the far side of the room. They'd both rolled up their shirtsleeves, and she found herself fascinated by the play of muscles on Logan's forearms, the bulges tightening the fabric around his biceps.

Ginny walked in from the kitchen, and her brown eyes sparkled with admiration as she whispered, "Well, I'm in love."

"It takes more than bulging biceps and brute strength to impress me," Cassie said just as quietly.

Ginny gave her a knowing look. "Uh-huh. Sure."

"Really."

"Whatever you say, Cass."

Saved from further defending her little white lie by the distant cries of her unhappy daughters, Cassie looped her arm through Ginny's. "Come on. You can go back to enjoying Hank's brawn later. Right now I need help getting the twins downstairs for lunch."

"I don't know what Hank has, but if he could bottle and sell it, I'd buy a whole case," Ginny said, looking over her shoulder at the men while Cassie pulled her along.

"I don't think you'll have to," Cassie whispered. "Unless I miss my guess, you'll get all the free samples you want."

"And I'll take all I can get." Grinning, Ginny added, "Just remember, I saw Hank first."

Climbing the stairs, Cassie laughed. "You're welcome to him."

I'm more attracted to Logan.

The unwarranted thought made her stumble. Now, where had that come from?

She shook her head to dislodge the silly notion. She was about as interested in Logan Murdock as she was in rotating the tires on a car.

Ten minutes later, Cassie had Chelsea and Kelsie strapped in their high chairs and had just removed the warmed baby food from the microwave when she turned to find Logan standing in the doorway, watching her.

"You didn't have to go to all this trouble," he said, referring to the huge bowl of beef stew on the table.

Cassie shrugged as she spooned the baby food into

divided plates and set them on the table. "We had to eat, and I like to cook." Turning back, she took a towel from the counter, opened the oven door and bent to remove a pan of freshly baked bread. "I hope you like what we're having."

"Uh…yeah, it's fine." The air in Logan's lungs stalled and he had to force himself to exhale.

Oh, he liked what she had, all right. Her loose khaki camp shorts were by no means tight, but bent over as she was, they clung to her shapely little backside and caused a certain part of his body to come to full alert. Damn! As bottoms went, the Widow Wellington had the best-looking rear he'd seen in a month of Sundays. Maybe ever.

When the babies slapped their trays and let out high-pitched squeals, she turned to grin at them. His heart stopped right then and there. Dimples. Cassie had tiny little dimples denting her porcelain cheeks. Why hadn't he noticed them yesterday?

Damn! Ever since he'd sat next to Rosie Collins in second grade, he'd been a sucker for females with dimples. And that didn't bode well. Not well at all.

The toothless grins the twins flashed back at their mother revealed they both had dimples, too. As far as little kids went, they were cute. Real cute.

Logan felt a chunk of the wall he'd carefully constructed around his heart fall away. The little girls almost had him wishing for kids of his own. But that was ridiculous. Having kids wasn't, and never would be, an option for him.

Sliding into the chair at the head of the table, he felt sweat pop out on his forehead and he cursed himself as nine kinds of a fool. So Cassie had a pretty smile, a shape that would tempt a eunuch and cute little kids. So what? She was trying to take over *his* ranch. He'd better not forget that.

"What do you lovely ladies have planned for this afternoon?" Hank asked, entering the kitchen with Ginny.

"I have to return the rented trailer before I'm charged for another day," Cassie answered. Logan watched her tie bibs around the twins' necks, then seat herself in the chair facing them.

"I'm driving down to Bear Creek for supplies. I could take the trailer back for you," Hank offered, holding Ginny's chair. He sat next to her. "By the way, do you think you could spare Ginny for a few hours this afternoon? I'd like to show her around town."

"I really should help Cassie," Ginny said. "She'll need me to watch the babies while she finishes the living room."

As distracted as he was by Cassie and her killer dimples, even Logan could detect the lack of enthusiasm in Ginny's voice.

He watched Cassie spoon lumpy-looking orange stuff into one twin's mouth, while she held a bottle for the other. No wonder the babies were slapping their trays. He would, too, if he had to eat that unappealing stuff.

"Don't be silly," Cassie said. "The girls will take a long nap after lunch. That should give me plenty of time to deal with the rest of the cobwebs and dust bunnies. If you have time when we get back, we'll buff the floors and polish the woodwork. If not, we'll tackle it tomorrow."

"Great," Ginny said happily. She smiled at Hank. "We won't be gone long."

Logan silently listened to the exchange. He wasn't at all happy about being left alone with Cassie. Even if Hank and Ginny didn't kill any more time in Bear Creek than it took to return the trailer and pick up some fencing supplies, it would be at least two and a half to three hours before they got back. And knowing the way Hank liked to visit with the guys down at the feed store, it could take even longer.

Hopefully, he could talk Cassie into taking her babies and going with Hank and Ginny. "Is there anything you need from town?" he asked. "Maybe you should go with them."

Cassie shook her head. "I have everything I'll need for a while."

"You'd better give it plenty of thought," Logan warned, taking a bite of the most bland beef stew he'd ever tasted. Somebody needed to teach the widow how to use the salt and pepper shakers. He took a drink of iced tea to wash the pasty stuff down before adding, "This isn't like St. Louis. We don't have a convenience store just down the block."

"I'm well aware that the last Wal-Mart we passed is over seventy-five miles from here," she said calmly.

He pointed at the babies. "What if you need something for those two? The closest store is the Rancher's Emporium and it's still a good forty miles away."

She stopped feeding the twins to glare at him. "I know how far it is between here and Bear Creek. And my daughters' names are Chelsea and Kelsie."

Logan couldn't stop his amused smile. "It sounds like you're reciting poetry."

"Round two, coming up," Hank said, shoving away from the table. "Ginny, I think that's our cue to mosey on out of here and let these two see if they can't work out some kind of a peace treaty."

Ginny looked uncertain. "Cassie?"

"Have a good time," Cassie said, her gaze never leaving Logan's.

"I'll be back in time to help with dinner," Ginny assured her, then hurried after Hank.

When the door closed behind them, Cassie left her place at the table to retrieve a washcloth. "So you don't like my daughters' names?"

"I can't say that I do or don't." Logan swallowed the last bite of his stew before adding, "I just think it's rather unusual the way they rhyme. That's all."

"A lot of people have twins with similar-sounding names." Cassie smiled. "I have one cousin who named her twin boys Shane and Sean, and another who named her fraternal twins Stephen and Stephanie."

"Twins run in your family?"

She nodded. "The Hastings have four sets in this generation alone."

Cassie felt him watch her every move as she washed Chelsea's face and hands, then removed the tray to unfasten the chair's safety strap. Glancing over her shoulder, Cassie smiled at the surprised look on his face.

"They have seat belts." He sounded amazed.

"Of course they do." Cassie lifted her happy daughter from the high chair. "All the baby furniture on the market these days is required to have safety features to keep infants from hurting themselves.''

''How could they do that?'' he asked skeptically. ''They're too little to do anything but make noise.''

Cassie laughed. ''You don't know the first thing about babies, do you?''

He shook his head and sounded quite proud of himself when he added, ''I've never been around one for longer than it took to walk away.''

''You've never held a baby?''

He shook his head. ''Nope.''

His smug expression was enough to make her decide it was past time for Logan Murdock's record to be broken. Biting the inside of her lip to keep from laughing, Cassie walked around the opposite end of the table and placed Chelsea against his wide chest. His hands automatically came up to close around the baby, just as she'd counted on.

''Hey, what do you think you're doing?''

Her grin widened at the panic she detected in his voice and the alarmed expression crossing his handsome features. ''I need someone to hold Chelsea while I clean up Kelsie,'' she lied. She turned to attend to the remaining twin. ''Since Ginny and Hank left, you've been elected to the position of my after-lunch helper.''

In truth, she'd worked out a very efficient system of managing the care of two infants by herself. But Logan didn't know that. And she wasn't about to enlighten him.

''What am I supposed to do with her?'' he asked, holding the baby at arm's length.

''Nothing. Just hold her.''

When Logan looked at the copper-haired infant, she waved a tiny fist at him and moved her chubby legs as if she was trying to ride a bicycle. He frowned. Was he doing something wrong?

The baby squirmed and he automatically shifted her back to his chest, to sit on his left forearm, while he splayed his right hand on her tiny back for support. Now, how did he know to do that? He wasn't sure, but it must have been what she wanted, because she made some kind of watery sound in the back of her throat and flashed him a grin. He couldn't help himself. He smiled right back.

As far as babies went, Cassie's kids were the cutest he'd ever seen. And the one he held certainly seemed happy enough. At least, she wasn't raising a ruckus.

But her grin suddenly faded and she stared intently at his face.

"Something's wrong with…" He paused. "Which one am I holding?"

"Chelsea."

"Okay, something's wrong with Chelsea," he said, hoping the baby didn't start screeching like a cat with its tail caught in a door.

"What makes you say that?" Cassie lifted the other baby from the high chair, swung the infant onto her hip, then turned to face him.

"She's giving me the evil eye."

When the baby reached out to touch his upper lip with tiny fingers, Cassie laughed. "She's fascinated by your mustache. She's never seen one before."

"Oh."

As quickly as her smile had disappeared, the baby's grin returned and she squealed delightedly.

"Does that tickle?" Logan asked.

He felt foolish as hell talking to a baby. But the movement of his mouth caused the little girl to giggle and pound on his face with a tiny fist. He couldn't help himself—he laughed out loud.

"It looks like Chelsea isn't the only one enjoying herself," Cassie said, grinning. "For a man who's never been around babies, you're a natural. I'll bet you'll be a great father some day."

Logan was mesmerized by Cassie's lyrical voice and the reappearance of her dimples; it took a moment for him to realize what she'd said. "No, I won't. I don't ever intend to get married, let alone have kids."

The tiny girl he held chose that moment to lay her head on his shoulder and burrow her little face into the side of his neck.

"That's a shame, because you really would be a good father," Cassie insisted. "Babies sense who they can trust and who they can't. If she didn't trust you completely, she'd be fussing instead of snuggling against you." Cassie pointed to his hand, rubbing small circles on Chelsea's back. "And you instinctively knew to do that."

Logan suddenly felt the need to run like hell. If the Widow Wellington thought she'd charm him into accepting the situation by having him hold a baby and flashing her killer dimples, she'd better think again.

What did he know about babies? Absolutely nothing. He most definitely *was not* father material. Not by a long shot. And that's just the way he intended it to stay. The way it had to stay.

A shiver slithered up his spine and made the hair on the back of his neck stand straight up. Two days ago, on his way back from his camping trip, he'd stopped by the Flying J ranch to see if Nate Jackson had seen any signs of a cougar, and Logan still couldn't believe the chaos he'd found there. Nate's wife, Rosemary, had gone on the warpath when he and Nate left muddy boot tracks on her newly mopped floor. Their three little girls ran from room to room whooping and hollering as if they were devil possessed and their new baby boy screeched like a banshee gone berserk.

Up until yesterday, his life had been damned near perfect and just the way he wanted—peaceful, quiet and female free. And when the loneliness got to be too much—when he wanted a woman's company—he could get in his truck and drive the forty miles down to Bear Creek and find an agreeable little filly in one of the local watering holes.

The operative phrase being *when he wanted*.

The best thing he could do would be to put as much distance as he could between himself, Cassie and her brood. And keep it that way.

"Here," he said, abruptly handing Chelsea back to Cassie. "I've got work to do."

Cassie watched Logan grab his hat from the peg by the door and slam out of the house.

She barely controlled the urge to laugh out loud. An eight-month-old baby girl had intimidated Logan Murdock, powerful cattle rancher, rugged outdoorsman and one of the finest specimens of a thirty-something male Cassie had ever been privileged to see.

Her breath caught as she remembered how much of that maleness she'd seen yesterday afternoon when she'd found him in the bathtub. She quickly walked into the dining room, where she'd set up the twins' playpen, and placed her happy daughters on the colorful mat to play. Fanning at the heat radiating from her cheeks, she turned on a baby monitor, then went back into the kitchen to clear the table.

If holding a baby was all it took to send Logan running, then she'd have to hand him one of the twins every chance she got. It was far safer to watch his retreating back than it was to have him around reminding her of his impressive attributes.

Four

It was well after midnight when Logan finally left the mare he'd been attending and walked to the house. He had no doubts Dolly could have dropped the foal without him being there. Or he could have assigned one of the other four men who worked for him to take over the maternity watch.

But Logan needed time alone, time to think things through and figure out what he was going to do next. That's why he'd skipped supper to stay with the mare. Only, he still hadn't been able to come up with any solutions, or a way to convince Cassie to leave the Lazy Ace.

He wanted—no, needed—her and her cute little kids off the ranch before any more damage was done to his peace of mind. It had taken him a lot of years and it hadn't been easy, but he'd reconciled himself to the fact that he was meant to live life alone. And he for damned sure didn't need Cassie stirring up longings that he'd locked away long ago.

Ten years back he'd seen the ranch through the eyes of a city woman, thanks to his college sweetheart, Andrea. She'd taken one look at the ranch—at how far it was from town—and hightailed it back to Denver and all the conveniences of the big city.

At first he'd been devastated. They'd been together from the time they'd met in their freshman year until they graduated, and he'd thought it would be forever. But as time passed, he'd realized she'd been right. Women just weren't cut out for the solitude and loneliness of the land he loved. Or, as in the case of his mother, the hard work.

Logan's chest tightened with sorrow and a twinge of guilt every time he remembered his mother and the circumstances surrounding her death. She'd taken ill and died because she'd jumped in to save him from drowning in an icy pond. He'd been eleven at the time, and Logan would never forget the profound way it had altered his life. It had been the first and last time he'd ever witnessed his father shedding tears. It had also been the beginning of the end of any kind of relationship they had as father and son.

Logan shook his head to dislodge the disturbing memories. No matter how badly he might want it to be different, a woman and a bunch of kids just had no place on the Lazy Ace.

Entering the house, he used the bootjack by the back door to remove his boots, then walked through the kitchen and down the dark hall in his sock feet. One step into the living room and he let loose a startled bellow as his feet flew out from under him. Reaching out, he grasped the rail of the staircase and narrowly escaped busting his butt. He tried to regain his footing, but he felt as if he was trying to walk on a sheet of ice. He'd forgotten all about Cassie's plan to buff the hardwood floor.

His feet back under him, Logan stood for a moment and sniffed the air. What was that smell? When he identified it as the unfamiliar scent of flowers, the hair on the back of his neck tingled.

"What the hell has she done now?" he groused, gingerly walking over to the end table by the armchair. He turned on the lamp, bathing the living room in a muted glow and highlighting the fruits of Cassie's labor.

Logan sucked in a sharp breath and felt as if he'd taken a sucker punch to the gut. Well, hell! He'd thought all she intended to do was clean the place. But she'd filled *his* living room with all kinds of frilly "woman" things.

Flowery, ruffled tablecloths draped the end tables all the way to the highly polished floor, and matching slipcovers draped the couch and chairs. Pillows in contrasting colors lined the back of the couch and made it look damned unappealing for a man to stretch out on.

But the biggest insult to the normally masculine room had to be the way she'd put puffy bows on everything. She'd even used them at the windows to tie back the prissy-looking curtains hanging in place of the tan drapes.

He glanced at the fireplace. What in hell had she done with Morty? Instead of the moose head, a picture of red, pink and yellow roses in a copper pot hung over the mantel. It was damned near enough to make a man puke.

When he noticed the small baskets, lined with lace, sitting at various locations around the room, he picked up the one on the end table. Staring at what looked liked crushed dried flowers mixed with weeds, he stuck his nose close and took a big sniff. He sneezed three times before he plopped it back on the table with a disgusted grunt. The damned stuff smelled just like that perfume old lady Watkins always wore when she came into the Rancher's Emporium. The cloud she left in her wake could choke a grizzly and could still be smelled for several hours after she'd left the store.

If Logan needed any more evidence that Cassie meant what she'd said about making the Lazy Ace her home, this had to be it.

"Nesting," he said disgustedly. He slipped and slid his way back across the room. "She's already started her damned nesting."

"Oh, it's you. What on earth were you yelling about?"

At the sight of Cassie standing on the bottom step of the staircase, her delicate hand resting on the rail, Logan swallowed hard and forgot anything he'd been about to say. The soft glow of sleep on her beautiful face and her strawberry-blond hair tumbling around her shoulders as if a lover had repeatedly run his hands through it were more arousing than anything Logan could ever have imagined. She'd obviously just gotten out of bed.

The thought of what she'd look like in *his* bed sent

heat sweeping through him faster than a streak of lightning and made his body tighten and strain against his fly. What was wrong with him? She wasn't wearing anything in the least bit provocative. Far from it. Her knee-length cotton nightshirt peeked out from beneath the hem of a robe that looked as if it had been made from an old bedspread, and bright purple balls of fur covered her feet.

Logan groaned. Hell's bells, the woman even managed to make ridiculous look good.

"Are you all right?" she asked, her obvious concern written all over her pretty face.

"Uh…yeah." He quickly turned around so she couldn't see the bulge in his jeans. The sudden movement made his feet slide, and it took all his effort to keep from landing flat on his ass. "How long did it take you to polish this floor?" he demanded, straightening himself.

"Not long. Isn't it beautiful the way it shined up?" she asked, sounding proud.

He grunted. "It's a hazard to walk on. I've damned near busted my as…butt twice in the last ten minutes."

"You're just not used to it." Cassie walked up behind him. "What do you think of the rest of the room? I brought the slipcovers, tablecloths and pillows with me, but I could order something in another color if you'd like."

She was so close it made his spine tingle. Glancing over his shoulder, he almost groaned aloud at her expression. She was eagerly waiting for him to tell her he thought the room looked wonderful, not that he thought she'd filled it with so many frilly ruffles and bows it looked as if a damned lace factory had exploded.

Shifting from one foot to the other, he finally settled on an answer he hoped she'd accept and not question further. "It looks a lot different than it did this morning. I can see you put a lot of work into it."

"Oh, it was a pleasure," she said, walking over to the couch to straighten one of the pillows. Her satisfied smile made a knot form in his stomach. "I'm really enjoying turning this place into a home. Do you like the potpourri scent I chose?"

"Potpourri?"

"In the baskets," she said, pointing to the crushed weeds. "I think it makes it more homey if things smell nice."

Logan felt as if the floor had dropped from beneath his feet. Well, there it was. She'd just the same as said she was turning *his house* into *her nest*.

His stomach churned and he searched for something to say. "What did you do with my moose?" he finally asked. There, that was a reasonable question, all things considered.

She wrinkled her pretty little nose. "I had Hank store it in the attic, along with the print of the poker-playing dogs and the neon beer sign."

Logan glanced to his left to find some kind of quilted thing hanging in place of the picture and a basket of ivy in place of his sign. Well, hell. He liked those dogs almost as much as he liked old Morty. And he'd had the neon sign since his college days.

Damn Hank's traitorous hide.

Cassie looked up at him, and the smile she gave

him just about knocked Logan off his feet. "They looked rather tacky and didn't go with the room's decor."

Instead of her insulting remark angering him, he lost all track of what had been said. How the hell was he supposed to keep his mind on what they were discussing when her green eyes twinkled with such enthusiasm, or she flashed those killer dimples at him?

He was damned tempted to haul her into his arms and kiss her until they were both senseless. Jamming his hands into the hip pockets of his jeans to keep from doing just that, he shrugged. "No, I don't guess they go with the new look."

"And I'm sure I'll be storing more in the attic once I've tackled the other rooms." She paused. "Are there any rooms you'd rather I not change?"

All of them. "I can't think of any," he said, shrugging. How was he supposed to think when she was close enough for him to smell that erotic cologne she always wore?

"Okay." She yawned and walked to the stairs. "By the way, I found a photo of you and your father. Would you like me to frame it and hang it in the hall with the rest of your family's pictures?"

Logan felt as if he'd been doused with a bucket of ice water. "No. Store it in the attic with the rest of the junk."

She gasped and turned back to face him. "But—"

"You heard what I said." Realizing how harsh his words must have sounded, he sighed heavily and rubbed the tension at the base of his neck. "Look, you might as well know that from the time I was eleven until the day he died, my father and I didn't get along.''

She reached out and placed her hand on his forearm. ''I'm sorry, Logan.''

The sound of her voice saying his name, the feel of her hand on his arm had his insides churning like a cement mixer. Before Logan could stop himself, he reached out and pulled her into his arms. Burying his face in her silky hair, he breathed in the scent of her. She smelled good. The combination of soft, sweet woman and that cologne of hers assaulted his senses and made his groin tighten with fierce need.

She pushed against his chest and leaned back to look up at him. ''What do you think you're doing?''

''Damned if I know,'' he answered honestly.

He had no idea why he'd taken her into his arms. Maybe he'd been too long without a woman. Maybe it had something to do with the loneliness and isolation he always felt when he thought of spending his life alone. Whatever the reason, all Logan knew for sure was how right her feminine curves felt pressed to his body, how he could feel the beat of her heart keep time with his own.

''I'm going to kiss you now, Cassie.''

''You shouldn't.''

''Probably not,'' he admitted. He brushed his mouth over hers. ''But I'm going to, anyway.''

It occurred to Cassie that she might have lost her mind, but she didn't say one single word to stop Logan from settling his mouth on hers. His soft mustache caused tingles of excitement to race through her and her heart to skip several beats. When he traced her lips, she opened for him without a second thought, and the feel of his tongue gently sliding into her mouth sent heat coursing through her veins.

Slowly, thoroughly, he explored, tasted and teased her into a thrilling game of advance and retreat. Never in her twenty-eight years had she ever been kissed with such mind-shattering tenderness, or such mastery. Her toes curled in her fuzzy-bunny slippers and an empty ache pooled deep inside her.

He pushed her chenille robe aside to cup the fullness of her breasts, then teased the tips with his thumbs. The feel of his hard arousal pressing into her stomach, the taste of his passion as he continued to kiss her and the arousing sensations he created as he chafed her tight nipples through the thin fabric made her knees buckle.

It had been so very long since she'd been the object of a man's desire. It felt good to be held again, to feel how much he wanted her.

"Easy, sugar," he said, catching her to him.

His softly spoken words vibrating against her lips and his mustache feathering over her sensitive skin made Cassie's insides feel as if they'd turned to warm, melted butter. He trailed kisses from her lips down to the hollow of her throat. Unable to stop herself, she brought her hands up to circle his neck and threaded her fingers in the thick black hair brushing the top of his collar.

The keening wail of an infant suddenly penetrated the sensual fog surrounding her, and Cassie tried to jerk from Logan's arms. "Please, turn me loose."

Without a word, he loosened his hold and stepped back. They stared at each other for endless seconds as if neither believed what had just taken place.

"One of your babies needs you," he said finally, breaking the silence stretching between them.

Confused by her actions and his, Cassie nodded and fled up the stairs without a backward glance. She couldn't—wouldn't—think about her behavior when Logan had taken her into his arms.

If she did, she'd have to admit just how attracted she was to the man, how his blatant sexuality made her body hum whenever she was near him. And that could prove disastrous to her plans of making the Lazy Ace a permanent home for herself and the twins.

"Hank?"

Logan entered the barn and, after allowing his eyes to adjust to the dim interior, looked around for his friend. A feminine giggle followed by a deep laugh filtered down from the loft overhead. He should have known Hank was with Ginny.

"Be right there, Logan."

"I'll be down by Nicoma's stall," Logan said, heading for the end of the barn.

Sitting on a bale of hay outside the mare's enclosure, Logan took his Resistol off and ran his hands through his hair. Kissing Cassie last night had been the biggest and most enjoyable mistake he'd ever made.

And he'd paid for it. Hell, he was still paying for it.

He'd spent a sleepless night, tossing and turning until just before dawn when he'd finally gotten up, dressed and left the house before Cassie had a chance to come downstairs to fix breakfast. It wasn't something he was proud of, but he just hadn't wanted to face her or the temptation she posed. That's why he'd gone to the bunkhouse for breakfast. But he'd been so irritable that his ranch hands Jock, Tucker and Ray had threatened to quit, and Gabe had gotten so thoroughly exasperated, he'd quit for the third time this week and refused to sit next to Logan at the table.

And all of his misery and uncharacteristic aggravation could be traced back to one source. Cassie Wellington.

What the hell had gotten into him last night, anyway? Why had he lost all control and given in to the temptation of kissing her?

All he'd succeeded in doing was losing an entire night's sleep and making himself miserable with wanting things he knew damned good and well he could never have.

He glanced up to see Ginny slip through the double doors and head for the house, while Hank picked straw from his hair and buttoned his shirt. When thoughts of spending time in the hayloft with Cassie invaded his mind, Logan gritted his teeth and swore.

"You look like hell," Hank said, swaggering up the barn aisle. "What did you do, go down to Buffalo Gals and tie one on last night?"

Logan shook his head. "I wish I had. I'd probably feel better." He jammed his hat on his head and met his friend's curious gaze. "I've got to get her off the Lazy Ace."

"Who?"

"You know who." Logan propped his forearms on his knees and stared at his boots. "She's turning the house into a spit-and-polished showplace that looks like a picture out of one of those women's magazines. And you can't walk on the floors. I damned near busted my ass twice last night trying to go upstairs to bed."

Sitting down beside him, Hank shrugged. "But it smells real nice."

Logan jerked his head up to meet his friend's philosophical gaze. "It smells like women."

"I know," Hank said, grinning.

Logan scowled, but the man's grin just widened. "I'm not going to be able to count on your help getting Cassie and her brood to leave, am I?"

"Nope." Hank laughed. "I'm determined to see that Ginny stays right here with me."

"You're setting yourself up for a fall, old buddy."

Hank's expression grew serious. "I don't think so, Logan. But at least I've got the guts to take that gamble. What about you?"

If they hadn't been friends since grade school, Logan would have hauled off and slugged the man. "Dammit, Hank, you know what happens to women out here. They either go stir-crazy or wind up dying well before their time."

Hank shook his head. "Look at old lady Watkins. She's eighty-four and still goin' strong." He paused, then in a low voice added, "What happened to your mom was just one of those freak things, Logan. There was no way of knowin' she'd catch pneumonia, or that a blizzard would keep your dad from gettin' her to town for help."

"She was only thirty-three. That's too young to die." Logan's gut twisted. "If we'd lived closer to town, she'd still be alive."

"You don't know that," Hank said reasonably. "People in town get sick and die just the same as folks who live out here." He took a deep breath, then met Logan's gaze. "Let it go. No matter what your dad said about her dying as a result of pulling you out of that pond, you didn't cause your mom's death."

Rationally, Logan knew Hank was right. But the thought of Cassie or one of her cute little kids becoming ill and him not being able to get medical attention for them made his stomach churn. "I've got to get her to see reason."

"You know, I think you're just feelin' a little crowded right now," Hank said. "You'll get used to it." He chuckled. "Who knows? You might even get to like the idea of havin' them around."

"No, I won't." Logan shook his head. His peace of mind just couldn't afford it. "And I for damned sure don't like the way she's decorating the place. I liked Morty hanging over the mantel."

Hank grinned. "I figured you'd take it hard about havin' Morty and the dogs stored in the attic." He paused, looking thoughtful. "You know, you do have another option."

"What's that?" Logan couldn't think of any, but he was more than willing to listen to any suggestion that would get Cassie and her family out of his house.

"Well, I'm the foreman of this spread, but I've always lived up here."

"It didn't make sense to have you live down there in the foreman's cabin when I've got five bedrooms.'' Logan brightened as he began to understand what Hank was driving at. "The cabin.''

Nodding, Hank smiled. "Yep. It needs some repairs, but I'd say we could have it ready in a few weeks.''

The more Logan thought about it, the better he liked the idea. It was only a quarter of a mile to the foreman's cabin. Cassie would be far enough away for his peace of mind, but close enough that he could keep an eye on her and the twins in case of an emergency. She could summon his help if she needed it, but not be underfoot all the time, driving him to the brink of insanity with her tempting little curves.

With any luck, she might even come to her senses well before the first snow and be safely back in St. Louis, content to receive her quarterly reports and dividend checks. Or better yet, maybe she'd decide she'd rather have the money all at once and take him up on his offer to buy out her share. That way, he'd still be able to carry through with his plan to give Hank an interest in the ranch.

While he worked on getting the cabin ready, he'd have something to keep his mind off Cassie and the way her kisses lit a fire in his blood and turned his brains to pure mush.

"That's perfect,'' Logan said, feeling better than he had in the past three days. He rose to his feet and walked determinedly up the barn aisle. "Come on, Hank. Let's get down there and see what it'll take to get it ready.''

"But what about the chores?'' Hank asked, following Logan out into the ranch yard.

"I'll pay the boys extra to take up the slack,''

Logan said, climbing into his truck. "You and I have a job to do. Now, get in the truck. I'd like to be down in Bear Creek by noon to pick up what we'll need to get started."

Careful of each step he took on the highly polished floor, Logan made it to the stairs without incident. It was getting close to midnight and he was bone tired, but plans to renovate the foreman's cabin were well under way and the satisfaction he felt was more than worth the fatigue.

He and Hank had spent the better part of the morning measuring, jotting down the supplies they'd need and cleaning out the dirt and cobwebs that had collected in the log structure over the years. After a trip down to Bear Creek, they'd returned with enough lumber and shingles to get started making the most immediate repairs. The rest of the supplies were on order and would be delivered in a few days.

As he passed Cassie's room, Logan wondered briefly how she'd spent her day. She'd pretty much finished ruining everything downstairs with all the lace and ruffles. All except for his office. He'd made sure to keep that door securely locked.

He shuddered to think what she'd do in there. Most likely the bear, lynx and rattlesnake would wind up joining Morty in the attic. Logan chuckled. Of course, to move them out she'd have to go back in the office, and after her reaction to the stuffed animals that first night, he seriously doubted that would happen.

Opening the door to his room, he shrugged out of his shirt and threw it at the chair, then flicked open the snap at the waistband of his jeans. He'd get a fresh set of clothes, take a quick shower, then get some sleep.

He started across the room to the dresser. Only, the dresser wasn't where it was supposed to be. "What the hell?"

He moved to reach for the lamp beside the bed, but hadn't gone more than a few feet before he banged his shin on a sharp corner and ran his toes into an immovable object. Pain shot through his foot and leg, and he hopped around cursing like a drunken sailor. When he finally found the edge of the bed to sit down and rub his throbbing toes and aching shin, he discovered it was on the opposite side of the room from where it was supposed to be.

Waving his arms around in the dark, Logan finally located the lamp on the bedside table and switched it on. He cut loose with a fresh wave of cusswords that would have blued the hair on every little old lady in the state of Wyoming and probably half of Montana.

"She's gone too damned far this time." He ground out the words, rising to his feet. First it was Morty and the dogs. Now this. She'd not only rearranged his furniture, she'd put some of those damned crushed weeds she called potpourri somewhere in the room. He couldn't see it, but he could damned well smell it.

What was next? Would she be trying to rearrange the plumbing in the bathroom tomorrow?

Gingerly putting weight on his injured foot, he limped out into the hall. It was time somebody told Ms. Busybody to leave things the hell alone.

Five

Cassie awoke to someone pounding on her door and bellowing like an enraged bull. Switching on the bedside lamp, she kicked the covers aside and jumped to her feet. If Logan Murdock woke the twins, she'd have his head on a silver platter.

Throwing open the door, she hissed, "Lower your voice before you wake the girls." She stopped short when she saw the dark scowl lining his brow. "Is something wrong?"

"You could say that." He gave her a tight smile. "You've gone too far this time, lady," he added, his voice sounding a lot like a growling animal.

She took a step back. "What do you mean?"

"First there was Morty and the dogs."

"M-Morty?"

"I let that slide." He advanced a step.

She retreated half a step. "Wh-what dogs?"

"But not this."

"What are you talking about?" she asked, side-stepping one of the twins' teddy bears lying on the hardwood floor. Had Logan slipped downstairs and hit his head? Was that why he was being irrational? Why did he think she'd know anything about some man named Morty and his dogs?

"You know damn good and well what I'm talking about," he said, moving forward.

"No, I don't," she said, retreating another step.

He advanced. "You invaded my personal space. What the hell made you think you could rearrange my bedroom?"

"You told me I could."

"Like hell I did." He started toward her again, but suddenly stumbled and, lunging forward, crashed into her, knocking her off her feet in a flying tackle.

Cassie had no time to react as Logan's arms closed around her a split second before they landed on the bed in an undignified heap. Flat on her back with him on top of her, she lay in stunned silence for several seconds as she tried to gather her wits about her.

All that registered was the fact that Logan's weight pressed her into the mattress, his hard muscles touching her from shoulders to knees. The feel of his bare chest against her cheek, the sound of his rather unsteady heartbeat beneath her ear and the mingled scents of leather and man assaulted her senses, making her traitorous body tingle to life.

"Are you all right?" he asked, leaning back to look down at her.

"Yes."

He glanced over the side of the bed. "What's a teddy bear doing in the middle of the floor?"

She blinked. How was she supposed to form a rational answer with his warm breath whispering over her cheek and his lips hovering just above hers? "It fell from the shelf…when you pounded on the door."

Logan looked down at the woman in his arms. Her soft body felt good beneath his. Real good. When her expressive green gaze met his, he groaned. Along with stunned disbelief and apprehension, he saw the same awareness that gripped him, watched it turn into the undeniable spark of desire as she stared up at him.

He knew for a fact that he'd lost what little sense he had left, but as the blood rushed from his brain to the region below his belt, he could no more stop himself from kissing her than he could keep the sun from rising in the east each morning. Besides, kissing Cassie was much more appealing than continuing to read her the riot act over a damned stuffed moose and rearranged furniture.

Lowering his mouth to hers, he heard her soft intake of breath, felt her body tense slightly beneath his. But when their lips met, she circled his neck with her arms and melted into him. At the small gesture of acceptance, fire streaked through him and he came to full erection. She might make him mad enough to chew nails in two, but he wanted her with a fierceness that knocked the wind out of him.

He savored her lips and memorized their softness, adding an urgency to the hunger building inside him.

When a tiny moan of pleasure escaped her, he accepted the invitation and pushed past her parted lips to explore her more completely. She tasted of minty toothpaste and sweet, willing woman.

Her tongue met his in a tentative mating, and Logan felt as if he'd been handed a rare gift. She'd never admit it, and maybe she didn't even realize it herself, but Cassie was letting him know without words that she wanted his kiss, wanted to taste his passion as much as he wanted the same from her.

He loosened his hold on her to run his hands along her sides to the swell of her breasts. Her thin night-shirt was the only barrier between them and he could feel her nipples peak in anticipation of his touch. The knowledge sent a fresh surge of need straight to his groin.

Rubbing the tight nubs with his thumbs, he kissed his way to the rapid pulse at the base of her throat. "Feel good, sugar?"

"Mmmm."

He lowered his head and touched first one taut peak, then the other with his tongue. Her nails scored his bare back and she moaned softly. Impatient to taste the puckered flesh without the hindrance of the thin cotton fabric, he reached down and lifted the tail of the shirt to expose her bare breasts to his appreciative gaze.

"Beautiful," he said, taking her into his mouth.

As he teased and coaxed her, she arched her back and threaded her fingers through his hair. Shifting his position, he pressed the hard ridge of his erection against her thigh, allowing her to feel what she did to him, how much she made him want her.

Never in his entire life had he been aroused faster or wanted a woman more than he did Cassie at that very moment. And not just physically.

Well, hell! Why did he have to have that grand revelation now? He had no business longing for the things Cassie made him want. Things he knew damned good and well he could never have.

Rolling to her side, he pulled her nightshirt down to cover her breasts, then sat up. "Look, I..."

What was he going to say? What could he say? He for damned sure wasn't going to tell her he was sorry, because for all the hell he was going through now, her soft flesh beneath his and her sweet taste on his lips were worth whatever torture he had to endure.

"I'll...uh, see you in the morning," he finally said, rising to his feet.

He didn't look back as he crossed the room. He couldn't. If he did, he wasn't sure he could walk away before he did something that both of them would end up regretting. And he couldn't bear the thought of Cassie having regrets about making love with him.

Cassie watched Logan walk to the door without a backward glance. He closed it behind him with a quiet click and only then did she manage to get her lungs to take in air again.

What in heaven's name had gotten into her? She'd never in her entire life been the passionate type. Nor had she ever questioned that lovemaking was anything but mildly pleasurable for a woman. Not even in the early days of her marriage when love was new and she'd been blinded to Stan's selfish nature had she felt such intense sensations or longed for more. But all Logan had to do was touch her and she seemed to lose every ounce of common sense she possessed and turn into a bundle of wanton need.

Her cheeks burned as she remembered clutching his head to her, reveling in the feel of his hot, wet mouth drawing deeply on her breast. Her nipples peaked and the coil in her womb tightened once again.

"Oooh," she moaned, crawling back beneath the covers. She curled into a ball as she fought the ache of unfulfilled desire.

She reminded herself that the girls' future depended on her keeping her head and not doing something stupid. Any involvement with Logan Murdock beyond their business partnership would be pure and absolute insanity.

But the memory of his hands on her body, his lips moving over her sensitive skin, kept her awake well into the night. When she finally did manage to drift off to sleep, she dreamed of a tall, dark-haired cowboy with hot, wild kisses and the touch of a sorcerer.

Cassie spooned the last bite of cereal into Chelsea's mouth and wondered for the hundredth time where Ginny and Hank were. Without the buffer they provided, breakfast had been a silent, uncomfortable affair. Logan had managed a formal "good morning" when he first came to the table, but he hadn't looked directly at her and he'd quickly fallen into silence as he ate.

How long could they avoid talking to each other?

Would they pretend what had taken place last night and the night before had never happened?

Her nerves on edge, Cassie jumped when Kelsie pounded on her tray. The baby was staring intently at Logan and holding her little arms out for him to take her.

"No, sweetie," Cassie said, wiping Kelsie's mouth. "Mr. Murdock's eating."

Logan looked up, and Cassie could feel his intense gaze watching every move she made. When she dropped the washcloth on the floor and had to rinse it in the sink before wiping off Chelsea, he set down his fork.

"Here. I'll hold her while you take care of the other one."

Cassie swallowed her surprise as she lifted Kelsie from the high chair and handed her to Logan. "Thank you." Turning back to wipe off Chelsea, she asked, "Have you seen Hank this morning?"

She unfastened the safety belt and settled the baby in her arms before turning to find a deep frown creasing Logan's forehead.

"No, I haven't."

At his harsh tone, Kelsie whimpered and her tiny chin wobbled.

His expression immediately changed and he brought the baby's hand up to tickle it with his mustache. "Sorry, sprite. I didn't mean to scare you."

Kelsie squealed happily and pounded on his face with her other hand. The sight made Cassie's insides ache.

The girls would never know what it was like to have a father. She swallowed around the lump in her throat. Unfortunately, even if Stan hadn't died in that car accident, it wouldn't have been any different. The girls still wouldn't have had a father. He'd made it perfectly clear that if she insisted on completing the pregnancy, he'd divorce her and never look back. And Cassie knew he'd meant every word he'd said.

Disturbed by the thought of what the twins were missing, Cassie didn't realize for a moment that Logan was speaking to her. "What was that?"

"I asked if you've seen your friend Ginny."

Cassie shook her head and headed for the hall. "I would imagine she's still in bed. Why?"

"If either one of you happen to see Hank, tell him I've already gone to work on that project we started yesterday." He followed her into the living room, where she'd placed a quilt on the floor. "Can you manage these two this morning?"

"Of course." She placed Chelsea on the colorful patchwork, then took Kelsie from him. "After we play for a while, they'll take a nap."

"I have work to do," he said. "If you need anything…" He paused, staring at her. "Where did you get that mark?" he demanded.

She reached up to touch the small red spot on the side of her throat. "I…uh, think it's irritation from—"

He swore. "It's a whisker burn." Running his hand across the back of his neck, he shook his head. "Look, I—"

Cassie's cheeks heated and she looked away. "Don't worry about it. It should fade in a couple of days."

Logan touched her chin with his index finger, lifting it so her gaze met his. "I'm sorry, Cassie. It won't happen again. I give you my word."

The intense look in his deep blue eyes made her heart twist. Why did it bother her that he was vowing not to kiss her again? Wasn't that what she wanted, too?

Dropping his hand, he stepped back, then stared at her for several long seconds. Just when she thought she'd melt from his intense scrutiny, he turned and headed for the door.

"Lunch will be ready at noon."

"Don't worry about lunch for me," he called over his shoulder. "I'll be down at the foreman's cabin until suppertime. Maybe longer."

When she heard his truck roar to life, she sighed. "Well, I guess that settles that." She looked down at her happy daughters. "Looks like we're on our own this morning, girls. At least, until Ginny finally decides to get up and greet the day."

Four hours later Cassie glanced at the clock, then at the stairs. She hated to bother Ginny, since she was technically on vacation. But the twins would be waking up from their naps soon and Cassie really could use help making lunch. She'd developed a slight headache and so far the tablets she'd taken hadn't relieved it.

Just as she made the decision to go upstairs and roust Ginny from bed, the phone rang. Hoping the sound hadn't disturbed the girls, Cassie grabbed it before it rang a second time.

"Lazy Ace Cattle Company."

"Hi, Cass."

"Ginny?" Cassie glanced at the stairs. So much

for her theory about Ginny sleeping in. "Where are you?"

"Cheyenne." Ginny sounded breathless and...happier than Cassie could ever remember.

"Is Hank with you?" she asked, already sure she knew the answer.

"Yes, he is." Ginny giggled. "Cass, Hank and I got married last night."

Cassie felt as if the floor tilted beneath her feet. "You did what?"

Ginny laughed. "You heard me."

"My God, Ginny, you've known him less than a week."

Her friend was silent a moment. "I know I haven't known Hank very long, but I really love him, Cass."

Cassie sighed. "Well, you know I'm happy for you. I'm just in shock."

"I'm sorry, Cass. I know I always said you'd be my maid of honor when I got married, but Hank swept me off my feet. Listen, I don't have time to talk right now. As soon as Hank gets back with breakfast—"

"It's time for lunch," Cassie said dryly.

"Oh, yeah. I suppose you're right," Ginny said, giggling. "Anyway, when Hank gets back, we're heading down to Denver for a short honeymoon. He wanted me to have you tell Logan that we'll be back in about a week." In the background, Cassie could hear someone pounding on a door. "Just a minute, darling. Listen, Cassie, I have to go. Take care and we'll see you in a week."

When the line went dead, Cassie stared at the phone for a full minute before placing the receiver back on its cradle. Ginny marrying Hank had been a huge surprise. But what shocked Cassie more than anything was the wave of longing that had coursed through her—was still coursing through her—at Ginny's announcement.

Hank had adored Ginny from the moment they met. What would it be like to be loved like that? To be married to someone who loved his spouse more than he loved himself?

She certainly hadn't had that with her late husband. Even if Stan had lived, their marriage wouldn't have lasted. Two days before he died in that car accident, he'd filed papers to divorce her.

But what would it be like if she and Logan were married? Would he be happy and content to be a good husband and father? Or would he be selfish and self-centered like Stan?

Something deep inside told her Logan wasn't like that. She had the feeling that once he gave his heart to a woman, he'd cherish her for the rest of his life. The thought increased the longing deep inside her.

Cassie shook her head to dislodge her wayward thoughts. She had absolutely no business wondering what marriage to Logan would be like. Or, for that matter, what it would be like to be married to any other man.

She wished Ginny and Hank all the best. But her marriage to Stan had taught her one very important lesson, and one that she'd do well to remember. Happily-ever-afters existed only in fairy tales.

Logan laid down the hammer to wipe the sweat from his brow with the shirt he'd removed earlier.

Tossing it on the tailgate of his truck, he stared at the tree line. He enjoyed the feel of the midday sun on his back, the heat easing his tired muscles. Hopefully, the unseasonably warm temperature meant they'd have a mild winter.

He glanced at the cabin. Whatever the weather, he fully intended to make the place as cozy as he could for Cassie and the babies. Not that they'd stay long. He had no doubt she'd have them all packed up and moved back to St. Louis by the first frost. But just in case, he'd make sure they were safe and warm in the little house.

Logan frowned. That sounded like something a man did for his family.

It was completely ridiculous, but the thought had him wondering what being married to Cassie would be like. Had she been happy with her late husband? She hadn't mentioned the man once since she'd arrived on the ranch. How long had he been dead? The guy couldn't have been gone for much more than a year, because the twins weren't that old. Had she come to terms with the man's passing? If the way she'd kissed him was any indication, he figured she had.

Just thinking about her response to his kisses had him halfway hard. And why didn't the idea of her and her little family leaving the Lazy Ace create the anticipation for him that it had a few days ago? Wasn't that what he wanted? Why had he lost the urgency he'd first felt when Hank mentioned renovating the foreman's cabin?

Shaking his head, Logan decided he'd better stop wondering about Cassie and concentrate on the present problem. It would be a hell of a lot safer than the answers he'd come up with to his speculation.

He sighed heavily. He still wanted to give Hank an interest in the ranch. But as long as Cassie refused to sell him her share, Logan couldn't do it. As it stood at the moment, he owned 50 percent. If he gave Hank anything, she'd hold controlling interest. And there was no way in hell Logan wanted that happening. She'd probably do something stupid like hang curtains in the windows of the horse stalls and try to braid the ends of the steers' tails.

Logan checked his watch. Hank still hadn't shown up. Where was the man, anyway? In all the years he'd known him, Logan could count on one hand the number of times that Hank had missed work. The first had been the morning after Nicoma stepped on his foot and Hank couldn't get his boot on. The second had been the day he'd attended the graveside services when Logan's dad had been buried.

"So this is what you've been working on."

His back to the lane leading to the cabin, Logan hadn't noticed Cassie or the tandem stroller she was pushing. Turning, he sucked in a sharp breath at the sight of her.

Damn, but she looked good. The sunlight turned her strawberry-blond hair to a warm reddish gold, making him want to thread his fingers through it, to feel it spill over his hands as he kissed her, made love to her. His body stirred to life and a fresh wave of sweat that had nothing to do with the warm temperature beaded his forehead.

Her blue tank top exposed enough flawless porcelain skin to make his mouth water and his jeans feel way too snug. But when she bent to check on the babies, her shorts stretched across her delectable little backside and Logan wondered what kept him from busting his fly.

"What are you doing here?" he asked, wincing at his blunt tone. He shifted in an effort to relieve some of the pressure from his painfully tight jeans.

When her smile faded, Logan felt like a prize jerk.

"I brought you lunch," she said, taking a small cooler from the back of the stroller.

"Sorry," he muttered. "I'm tired and more than a little irritated with Hank."

Their hands touched when she passed the insulated container to him, and a jolt of electrified desire shot straight up his arm and exploded in the pit of his belly. He was in trouble. Big trouble. And if he had any sense, he'd jump into the truck and drive like hell down to Buffalo Gals Bar and Grill in Bear Creek.

But he had a feeling none of the willing little fillies he'd find there could take care of the ache building inside him. No. Only one woman held the scratch for his itch and she was standing right here in front of him.

"Speaking of Hank, I heard from Ginny about an hour ago." She looked as if there was more to tell.

Opening the cooler, he removed a sandwich and can of soda. "And?"

"She and Hank won't be back for a week."

Logan stopped unwrapping the sandwich for a moment to look at her. "Why? Where the hell are they?"

She took a deep breath, and he had a feeling he

wasn't going to like what she had to say. "They got married last night down in Cheyenne."

He froze with the sandwich halfway to his mouth. "They did what?"

"They eloped," she said. "They're on their way to Denver right now for their honeymoon."

Staring at Cassie, Logan felt reality begin to sink in. He and Cassie were going to be stuck in the same house for the next week. Alone.

All alone.

His graphic curse made her eyes widen. "Could you please watch your language? I'd rather not have the twins' first words be something like *that*."

"Sorry."

He ran a hand across the back of his neck to ease his tightening muscles. If he could have gotten his hands on Hank at that very moment, Logan would cheerfully have choked the man. Couldn't Hank have postponed the honeymoon until after they got the foreman's cabin finished and Cassie and her babies moved in?

It would have been a damned sight easier on all concerned if he had. And especially for Logan. He was already having enough trouble keeping his hands off Cassie. What would happen now that Hank and Ginny weren't there to distract him?

His vivid memory replayed the previous night's events. Cassie lying soft and warm beneath him on the big four-poster bed, the sweet taste of her as his lips explored hers. Her breasts had filled his hands to perfection and her nipples had puckered immediately at his touch.

Sweat trickled from his temple down the side of

his face to his jaw. She was staring back at him, and he could tell she wasn't as unaffected by him as she'd like to let on. Her gaze caressed every inch of his bare chest and her hand had trembled when she'd handed him the cooler. He'd loved every minute of her inspection of his body, felt deeply satisfied by her inability to conceal her attraction.

"Whose house is this?" Cassie asked.

She was looking closely at the front of the little cottage. Given her penchant for rearranging things, she probably thought the door would look better in a different place.

"It's the foreman's house," Logan answered, feeling guilty. She had no way of knowing he intended to move her and the babies into it.

"You knew Hank and Ginny were getting married?" She sounded hurt by the idea that she hadn't known about her friend's nuptials.

He shook his head. "It was as big a surprise to me as it was to you."

"Then why are you working on it?"

"Hank suggested it," Logan said, not wanting to reveal his plans.

Cassie grinned at him, and he almost groaned at the reappearance of her dimples. "I guess now we know why he made the suggestion. He was planning to spend time alone with Ginny."

Logan frowned. What Cassie had said made sense. When Hank had suggested they work on the house, he'd planned all along to take up residence with Ginny in the cabin, and he'd suckered Logan into helping. The next time he saw Hank, Logan fully intended to skin him alive, then nail his ornery hide to the barn.

Logan closed his eyes and shook his head. Now he'd be stuck with Cassie in *his* house. Alone.

His life was going to be pure hell and he'd be lucky to have a lick of sense left by the time she decided to pack up and move on.

Six

By that evening, Cassie's headache still pounded unmercifully and her stomach had begun to churn. Every muscle and joint in her body ached and she alternated between chills and feeling as if she was burning up. When she bent over to remove a casserole from the oven, the throbbing in her head increased and she swayed as a wave of dizziness swept over her.

"Are you all right?" Logan asked, hanging his hat on a peg beside the back door. Looking concerned, he walked up to her. "Your cheeks look like somebody slapped you."

She tried to shake her head, but winced at the discomfort the movement created. "It's just a little headache. I'll be fine. Dinner is almost ready, if you'd like to wash up."

He reached out and placed his large palm on her forehead. "Damn! You're burning up." Grabbing a couple of pot holders from the counter, he took the casserole from her and set it on the table, then, pulling out one of the chairs, he said, "Sit down."

"I don't have time—"

"Dammit, I said sit." He disappeared down the hall, only to return in a few minutes with a thermometer. "Open up," he ordered.

"I have a more modern ther—"

He slipped the thin glass stick into her mouth before she could finish telling him about the nifty little instrument she used for the twins. All he'd have to do was stick that to her ear and they'd know what her temperature was in seconds.

"Now, keep your mouth shut for a few minutes so we can see just how high your fever is running." He propped his hands on his lean hips. "Where are the babies?"

Cassie removed the thermometer. "In the—"

"Put that back in your mouth."

"I can't answer you with—"

"Just point."

If he thought his scowl would intimidate her, he was sadly mistaken. She felt too bad to care. "They're in the playpen in the living room."

He took the thermometer from her and stuck it back into her mouth. "Will they be okay for a few minutes? Just nod or shake your head," he added hastily.

She nodded and watched him disappear back down the hall. If she hadn't felt as if death would be a blessing, she'd wonder why he was overreacting. But at the moment she couldn't concentrate on anything but how badly her head pounded and how much her muscles ached.

When he returned he smiled. "They're both sleeping." He removed the thermometer and held it up to view the reading. "Damn! Your fever is over a hundred and three. We'd better get you to bed."

"No." She tried to get up, but her legs felt like limp noodles and she ached all over. "I've got too much to do."

"Like what?"

She sighed tiredly, and with great effort finally managed to rise from the chair. "I have to finish dinner, feed and bathe the girls, then put them to bed and wash a load of clothes."

Catching her around the waist, Logan supported her as he ushered her toward the stairs. "Don't worry about the twins. I'll see that everything is taken care of."

She thought he sounded a little too confident for a man who'd never cared for children before. "You don't know what to do."

He chuckled. "It can't be *that* hard. I'll figure it out."

Too tired to argue, Cassie nodded and let him help her to her room. If she'd felt better, she might have cared that he had to help her change into her nightgown, but at the moment she was too sick to give modesty a second thought. The last traces of her energy expended, she crawled into bed and shivered as the cool sheets met her heated skin.

Once Logan tucked the covers under her chin, he brought her a glass of water, a couple of aspirin and a cowbell. "Don't worry about a thing," he said, supporting her while she took the tablets. He lowered her to the pillows, then pointed to the cowbell. "If you need me, ring that."

"Okay," she said, hardly recognizing her own voice. She sounded like a very tired old lady.

Logan looked extremely worried as he stared down at her. "Are you sure you'll be all right?"

She nodded, but couldn't seem to make her voice work. She was simply too tired.

He brushed her hair back from her heated face and laid a cool damp washcloth on her forehead. "I'll see the babies are well cared for. You just rest and get better. I'll be up to check on you a little later."

Cassie nodded again. Her eyes felt as if they had lead weights on them. She should warn him about Chelsea's inclination to spit baby food everywhere and Kelsie's habit of splashing bathwater. She should also tell him how to fasten the tapes on the girls' diapers. But as he headed back down the hall, her eyes closed and she felt herself drifting off into an exhausted sleep.

Logan cursed a blue streak as he hung up the phone. The doctor who visited the clinic down in Bear Creek was only in on Thursdays, and this was Friday. If only Cassie had come down with the flu a day earlier, Logan could have gotten her in to see the doctor. The physician's assistant had given him instructions on the care of an influenza patient and he hoped she knew what she was talking about. She'd also scared the hell out of him when she'd given him a list of symptoms for pneumonia and cautioned him to watch for signs of complications.

He closed his eyes and took a deep breath. Cassie was going to be okay. He refused to believe otherwise. As long as he had breath left in his body, he wouldn't allow it to be a repeat of what had happened to his mother.

He made another trip upstairs to check on Cassie and assure himself she was resting comfortably. Her skin was a little cooler to the touch and he took that as a good sign.

Heading back to the kitchen, Logan went straight to the phone and dialed the bunkhouse. He wasn't fool enough to think he could handle a sick woman and two babies by himself. He needed help.

"Could you come up to the house?" Logan asked when Gabe Morris answered on the third ring. He would have demanded to know why it had taken Gabe so long to answer, but Logan couldn't afford to annoy the man at this stage of the game. Of all his men, Gabe was the only one who might have experience with children.

"What kinda mood are you in?" Gabe asked, sounding as if he still hadn't forgiven Logan for being so irritable lately.

Logan sighed heavily. "Look, I told you yesterday I was sorry. Now, get up here."

"Okay, boss." The man paused. "But you'd better be in a good mood or I'll quit."

"You won't have to. I'll fire you if you don't get the lead out of your ass and get up here," Logan said, hanging up the phone.

When Gabe showed up five minutes later, Logan

made sure he greeted the man with a smile. "I need your help, Gabe. Mrs. Wellington is sick and I need you to take care of her little girls while I—"

"No way, boss," Gabe said emphatically. The man suddenly looked like a trapped animal. Holding his hands up, he started backpedaling. "I don't know nothin' 'bout babies, 'cept for the bovine kind. And that's just the way I intend to keep it."

"But you said your sister has kids," Logan said reasonably.

"Well, my brother-in-law owns a movie theater up in Casper, too. But that don't make me a movie star," Gabe shot back. He quickly backed his way to the door. "You're on your own with this one, boss."

"I'll give you an extra week's pay," Logan offered, feeling desperate as he watched the man step out onto the porch. When Gabe shook his head, Logan tried again. "Make that two weeks' pay."

"Nope." Gabe turned and fled down the steps. "There ain't enough money in the state of Wyoming to get me to take care of them babies."

"You're fired," Logan shouted to the cowboy's retreating back.

Gabe kept going. "You can't fire me. I quit."

"You quit yesterday and the day before."

"Yeah, and you fired me last week and the week before that," Gabe said, breaking into a jog. "See you in the mornin', boss."

Logan watched his only hope for help disappear around the corner of the barn at a dead run. One of these days he was going to fire Gabe for real, he thought sourly.

The sound of an impatient infant, followed closely by a second baby's angry cry, sent a shiver slithering up Logan's spine as reality hit with the force of a wrecking ball. He was solely responsible for the care of two baby girls and one extremely ill woman.

Thoughts of his own mother and the illness that had claimed her life once again invaded his mind. What if Cassie had something worse than the flu? Would he be able to get her to a doctor in time?

Sweat beaded his forehead and he took a deep breath. It was early September, not February, and the chances of them being trapped in a blizzard were pretty damned slim this time of year.

No. Nothing was going to happen to Cassie. He wouldn't allow it. If he had to, he'd walk through hell and back, but Cassie was going to be all right.

He ground his back teeth. All of this was Hank's fault. If he hadn't taken Cassie's friend and eloped, Ginny would be here to take charge. Any fool knew that women were better at these things than men.

The crying increased in volume and he heard the distant sound of a cowbell clanging. Straightening his shoulders, Logan took a deep breath and headed down the hall to deal with the three females demanding his attention.

Twenty minutes later he was feeling pretty good about the way he was coping. He'd assured Cassie he had everything under control and had managed to strap the twins in their high chairs without incident.

You can do this, Murdock.

Most of it was common sense stuff. As long as he kept that in mind, everything should be okay.

Filling one of the tiny spoons with food, he held

it to one of the little girls' mouths, while he juggled a bottle for the other one. He smiled. This wasn't as difficult as he'd thought it would be.

A split second later he frowned as he looked down at the orange spot on his shirt, then at the baby who'd put it there. "I take it you don't like carrots?"

The chubby little girl treated him to a toothless grin and slapped her hands down in the divided dish he'd placed in the middle of her tray. Mushy baby food flew in all directions.

"Well, hel...heck," he muttered, adjusting his language for young ears. Now he knew why he'd never seen Cassie place the baby dishes within the twins' reach.

By the time Logan had the two babies fed, the three of them were wearing more food than he'd gotten them to eat and he had a whole new respect for Cassie. She made feeding the twins look easy. It wasn't. Not by a long shot.

Wiping the nasty mush from his shirt and face, he turned to do the same with the babies. Only, that proved more difficult than he'd anticipated. It was damned hard to clean a moving target, he decided as the twins turned their heads, rocked back and forth and grabbed at the washcloth. Giving up, he managed to get them both out of the high chairs, then tucked one under each arm and headed for the bathroom upstairs. There was no way he'd attempt to clean the kitchen until after he got the twins in bed for the night.

Once he'd filled the tub with a couple of inches of warm water, he stripped both babies and proceeded to try to bathe them. Since they didn't smell like regular bath soap, he opted to just rinse them off with the clear water. Cassie probably used something special just for babies, but he didn't know what it was and he wasn't about to disturb her to find out.

Pleased that things seemed to be going along pretty well with the bath, Logan wasn't prepared when one of them started thrashing her legs and slapping the water with her little hands. The other one soon joined in and Logan groaned. He was as wet as they were and the bathroom floor looked like a small lake.

Damn! Now he'd have to mop up the bathroom as well as clean the kitchen.

Wrapping the two babies in a huge bath towel, he took them into the room where Cassie had set up their cribs and placed a twin in each. Now what? He'd seen her put diapers on the girls, but never intending to perform the task himself, he hadn't paid any attention as to how she'd done it or what she'd used to make them stay on.

A sudden thought had him running downstairs with a smile on his face. Feeling quite proud of himself, he returned to the twins' room with a large roll of tape.

"When in doubt, duct it," he said triumphantly, grabbing a couple of diapers from the fancy little holder hanging in one corner of the room. "Now, where's that white stuff your mom sprinkles on before she slaps these things in place?"

While he searched for the powder, the tiny girls crawled to the rails of their cribs, pulled themselves to a standing position and made baby noises in answer to his question.

GIFTS from the Heart

Play and you can get **2 FREE BOOKS** and a **SURPRISE GIFT!**

GIFTS from the Heart

Play Gifts from the Heart and get 2 FREE Books and a FREE Gift!

HOW TO PLAY:

1. With a coin, carefully scratch off the gold area at the right. Then check the claim chart to see what we have for you — **2 FREE BOOKS** and a **FREE GIFT** — **ALL YOURS FREE!**

2. Send back the card and you'll receive two brand-new Silhouette Desire® novels. These books have a cover price of $3.99 each in the U.S. and $4.50 each in Canada, but they are yours to keep absolutely free.

3. There's no catch. You're under no obligation to buy anything. We charge nothing —**ZERO** — for your first shipment. And you don't have to make any minimum number of purchases — not even one!

4. The fact is, thousands of readers enjoy receiving books by mail from the Silhouette Reader Service™. They enjoy the convenience of home delivery... they like getting the best new novels at discount prices, **BEFORE** they're available in stores...and they love their *Heart to Heart* subscriber newsletter featuring author news, horoscopes, recipes, book reviews and much more!

5. We hope that after receiving your free books you'll want to remain a subscriber. But the choice is yours — to continue or cancel, any time at all! So why not take us up on our invitation, with no risk of any kind. You'll be glad you did!

A surprise gift

FREE!

We can't tell you what it is... but we're sure you'll like it! A

FREE GIFT!

just for playing **GIFTS FROM THE HEART!**

NO COST! NO OBLIGATION TO BUY!
NO PURCHASE NECESSARY!

PLAY GIFTS from the Heart

Scratch off the gold area with a coin.
Then check below to see the gifts you get!

YES! I have scratched off the gold area. Please send
me the 2 Free books and gift for which I qualify. I understand I
am under no obligation to purchase any books as explained
on the back and on the opposite page.

326 SDL DNSJ   225 SDL DNSE

FIRST NAME	LAST NAME

ADDRESS

APT.#	CITY

STATE/PROV.	ZIP/POSTAL CODE

 2 free books plus a surprise gift

2 free books   1 free book

The Silhouette Reader Service™ — Here's how it works:

Accepting your 2 free books and gift places you under no obligation to buy anything. You may keep the books and gift and return the shipping statement marked "cancel." If you do not cancel, about a month later we'll send you 6 additional books and bill you just $3.34 each in the U.S., or $3.74 each in Canada, plus 25¢ shipping & handling per book and applicable taxes if any.* That's the complete price and — compared to cover prices of $3.99 each in the U.S. and $4.50 each in Canada — it's quite a bargain! You may cancel at any time, but if you choose to continue, every month we'll send you 6 more books, which you may either purchase at the discount price or return to us and cancel your subscription.

*Terms and prices subject to change without notice. Sales tax applicable in N.Y. Canadian residents will be charged applicable provincial taxes and GST.

If offer card is missing write to: Silhouette Reader Service, 3010 Walden Ave., P.O. Box 1867, Buffalo NY 14240-1867

BUSINESS REPLY MAIL
FIRST-CLASS MAIL   PERMIT NO. 717-003   BUFFALO, NY

POSTAGE WILL BE PAID BY ADDRESSEE

SILHOUETTE READER SERVICE
3010 WALDEN AVE
PO BOX 1867
BUFFALO NY 14240-9952

NO POSTAGE
NECESSARY
IF MAILED
IN THE
UNITED STATES

Locating the plastic container, he twisted the cap and stopped short at the smell. "Well, I'll be dam...danged," he said incredulously.

The scent he found irresistible, the one that made him want to take Cassie in his arms and cradle her to him, wasn't cologne at all. It was baby powder. But on Cassie the stuff smelled as exotic as expensive perfume.

Logan didn't have time to dwell on his discovery. He needed to get the babies' bottoms covered before they did something else he'd have to clean up.

With a lot of effort, and taking at least twice the amount of time it took Cassie, Logan had the diapers in place, the sides secured with strips of duct tape and tiny pink T-shirts pulled on both girls. He watched as they began to blink and yawn. A few minutes later they were both sleeping peacefully.

And he felt as if he'd just competed in a triathlon.

But his job wasn't finished. He still had to deal with the cleanup.

After quickly mopping up the water on the bathroom floor and draining the tub, Logan checked on Cassie, then headed back downstairs to face the mess in the kitchen. His respect for Cassie and the chores of motherhood she performed with such ease had jumped several notches in the past couple of hours and was still rising.

The evening hadn't been easy, but it had given Logan a glimpse of what fatherhood was all about. He smiled. One of the twins—he still couldn't tell them apart—had giggled delightedly when he'd let her feed him some of her pudding, and the other one had laid her head on his shoulder and hugged his neck when he'd finished pulling her T-shirt over her head.

Taking care of the babies had been hard work, but he'd found himself enjoying it. He frowned. Unfortunately, he'd also found himself pondering things he had no business thinking about.

As he sponged baby food from the floor and high chairs, an empty ache settled deep in his chest. Even though he recognized it as pure insanity, it didn't ease the longing, or keep him from reflecting on what it would be like to be part of Cassie's little family.

When Logan walked into her room a day and a half later, Cassie propped herself up against the pillows. The past couple of days had been a blur, but she was beginning to feel as if she might just survive after all.

"How are the twins?" she asked anxiously. She hadn't dared be around them for fear they might catch the flu, and she missed them terribly.

Logan grinned and pointed to his shirt. "Just fine."

She smiled at the spots on his chambray shirt—water and something yellow. "I see you've fed and bathed them."

He nodded as he set a tray of food on the bedside table. "And they're down for the night." He paused as he glanced down at the front of his shirt. "You know, you could have warned me that one of them doesn't like carrots, squash or peas and the other one likes water sports."

Cassie laughed and reached for the bowl of chicken soup he'd brought her for supper. "It's not that Chelsea doesn't like those vegetables. She just likes playing while she eats. It's like a game for her. And Kelsie absolutely loves being in water."

"I know," he said dryly. "I predict she'll be an Olympic swimmer."

"Could be," Cassie said, smiling. She took a sip of the rich chicken broth. "Mmmm, this is good."

"I opened a can of soup this time, instead of having Tucker make it," Logan said, chuckling. "If he doesn't stop being so vain about how he'd look in glasses, I'll have the skinniest cowhands in Albany county."

She laughed. "Or they'll all quit because you're starving them." She took a sip of the orange juice he'd insisted she drink with every meal. "You know, I've been thinking I'd like to have a celebration dinner when Ginny and Hank get home."

Cassie felt a pang of longing every time she thought of her friend finding the man of her dreams, but quickly tamped it down. She wished Ginny and Hank nothing but the best in their marriage. "Do you think the men down at the bunkhouse would like to join us?"

"I'm sure the guys would like that idea a lot." Logan grinned. "It will be one night they won't have to eat Tucker's cooking."

Remembering how Tucker's beef soup had tasted, she nodded. "I can't really say I blame them." She took another sip of juice, then placed the empty glass back on the tray. Yawning, she leaned back against the pillows.

"Feeling any better today?" Logan asked, sitting on the bed beside her.

"Yes, but I tire easily," she said, distracted by his presence. Somehow it seemed extremely intimate having him sit on the bed beside her, carrying on a conversation about ordinary, everyday things.

He reached out and touched her cheek with the back of his hand. "You don't seem to be running a fever this evening. That's a good sign."

She caught her breath at the feel of his skin against hers. She might not be running a fever, but her temperature was definitely going up just from his touch. She must be getting well.

When his gaze caught and held hers for several long seconds, she became very conscious of the way she must look. No doubt her nose was cherry-red, her eyes bloodshot and her skin tone a sickly pale. Not exactly the stuff men's dreams were made of. But from the look in his eyes it didn't appear he was put off by her obviously haggard appearance.

"Have you heard from Hank or Ginny?" she asked, looking down at her hands. If she hadn't broken eye contact she might have drowned in his deep blue gaze. Glancing back up, she discovered he looked as disconcerted as she felt.

He cleared his throat. "They'll be home day after tomorrow." Rising from the side of the bed, he picked up the tray. "Do you need anything else before I go back downstairs?"

"No, I'll be fine." When he nodded and turned to leave the room, she added, "Thank you for taking such good care of the girls...and me."

He turned back, and she could have sworn he looked wistful and a little sad. "Believe me, Cassie. It was my pleasure."

* * *

Logan watched his men congratulate Hank and Ginny on their recent marriage, then file into the kitchen on the way back to the bunkhouse to thank Cassie for including them in the celebration. Each one had been on his best behavior. Even ornery old Gabe.

From the kitchen door Logan watched Cassie say goodbye to the men, then move around the kitchen putting away leftovers, loading the dishwasher and laughing with Ginny. Cassie had recovered from the flu and resumed her normal routine several days ago, but he still intended to keep a close eye on her—to make sure she didn't do too much too soon. But the truth was, he just liked watching her.

"Enjoyin' the scenery as much as I am?" Hank asked, coming to stand beside him.

"I'm just making sure Cassie doesn't overdo things," Logan said automatically.

"Uh-huh, sure." Hank's expression told him the man didn't believe Logan's flimsy excuse for a minute. "What do you say we go into the study, while the women get things cleaned up?"

Lifting a brow, Logan asked, "Don't you want to spend the evening with your bride?"

Hank grinned. "Oh, I don't intend to be away from her for very long. But I have something I need to talk over with you."

Logan nodded and headed toward the living room. "Let me check to make sure Chelsea and Kelsie are doing okay in the playpen."

"You got kind of attached to those little girls while Ginny and I were gone, didn't you?"

"I'm just helping Cassie out," Logan said. He hated the defensive tone of his voice almost as much as he hated the smirk on Hank's face.

Fortunately, Hank had the good sense not to comment further as they walked into the study. Logan would have hated having to deck his best friend when he had just returned from his honeymoon.

Lowering himself into the chair, Logan leaned back and propped his boots on the edge of the desk. "So what have you got on your mind?"

Hank's expression turned as serious as Logan had ever seen it. "Have you talked to Cassie about movin' into the foreman's place yet?"

"No."

"Good." Hank stared at his boots for several long seconds before he met Logan's gaze. "Don't get me wrong. I really appreciate you invitin' me and Ginny to stay here. But we've been talkin'. We'd like to move into the cabin as soon as it's finished."

"After Ginny called to say you two were married, I figured out you had this in mind when you suggested we work on it," Logan said, nodding.

He understood Hank wanting to be alone with his wife. But what Logan couldn't quite grasp was the sense of relief filling his soul. Cassie and the babies would be staying right here in the house with him.

"Glad you understand." Hank grinned. "How much more work will we have to do before it's ready?"

"We still have to install the kitchen cabinets and sink. And we'll have to replace the plumbing and wiring." Logan shrugged. "I'd say we could have it ready in about a month, maybe a little sooner if everything we ordered gets here on time.''

"Perfect.'' Hank's grin could have lit a small city. "We've already started tryin' for a baby.''

At Hank's announcement, envy sliced through Logan. But he did his best to conceal it. He found himself wishing for things to be different, wishing that he and Cassie were the ones trying to create a baby together. And that scared the hell out of him.

He'd never wondered what it would be like to watch a woman grow large with his child, lay his hand on her swollen belly and feel the baby move. But he suddenly envisioned how Cassie would look pregnant, and sweat popped out on his upper lip, while a shiver snaked its way up his spine.

Managing a smile, he said, ''Congratulations. I hope it looks like Ginny and not you.''

"That's what I'm hopin', too.'' Laughing, Hank rose to leave. "I think I'll go find my wife and continue our honeymoon.''

As Hank crossed the room to the door, Logan made a split-second decision. "Hank, do you think you could watch things around here for a couple of days?''

"Sure. Why?''

"I'm thinking about taking a trip up into the mountains to check on Samson,'' Logan said.

Hank nodded. "Need to do some thinkin'?''

Logan didn't try lying his way out of it. Hank knew him too well. "Yeah, I do.''

"What time you leavin'?''

"I'd like to get an early start.'' Logan left his chair

and followed Hank out into the hall. "I'll probably leave around daybreak tomorrow."

"I hope you get the answers you're lookin' for," Hank said, clapping Logan on the shoulder.

"I do, too, Hank," Logan said as he watched his friend head for the kitchen to find Ginny. "I do, too."

Seven

When the back screen door slammed shut, Logan looked over the horse he was saddling, expecting to see Hank. Instead, he watched Cassie coming across the yard toward him. She looked good in the pale light of dawn. Damned good.

But he couldn't remember a time since he'd met her that she hadn't. Even when she'd been ill, she'd looked good to him. He'd seen her at her worst and he'd still wanted her. Wanted to take care of her. That bothered him and was the reason he was heading up into the mountains.

As she approached, his body stirred and he bit back a curse. He was in deep trouble if all it took for him to get hard was her walking toward him. He thanked the good Lord above that he was standing on the other side of Dakota. At least he'd be able to hide the fact that he was aroused as long as he kept the horse between them.

"Where's my horse?" she asked, walking up to him.

His mouth dropped open. "Your horse?"

"Yes, my horse." She smiled, flashing those killer dimples, and he felt his insides catch fire and his stomach tighten. "I'm going with you."

Logan felt his world tilt and every nerve in his body come to full alert. "No, you're not."

Her smile disappeared. "Yes, I am."

She ran her hand down Dakota's gray neck, and Logan found himself wishing she'd run her hands down his body. He had to make himself concentrate on the rest of what she was saying.

"I want to see all of my inheritance. Besides, it can be dangerous up in the mountains. You shouldn't be going alone, and it's not fair for Hank to have to leave Ginny so soon after getting married."

Logan would bet everything he had that her last two statements were almost word for word right out of Hank's mouth. If Logan could have gotten his hands on the man at that moment, he'd have beaten the living tar out of him, then choked what was left of his sorry carcass for good measure.

"Don't worry about me," Logan said, adjusting the saddle girth. He tried to make his tone as reassuring as possible. "I've been traveling these mountains by myself since I was twelve years old, sugar. I know them like the back of my hand."

She nodded. "Then you'll be the perfect guide."

"You need to stay here with Chelsea and Kelsie," he said, turning to load the packhorse.

"Hank and Ginny have offered to take care of the girls." Her smile returned. "They said it would be good practice for them."

Logan stopped loading the packs to look directly at her. That was a big mistake, he decided. She looked so damned sweet and tempting that it took all of his resolve to shake his head. "I'm not taking you with me, Cassie."

"Yes, you are."

"*No,* I'm not."

Her silence gave him a moment of hope that she was about to give up. Then, walking around Dakota to him, she did the one thing he couldn't resist. She touched him.

"Please, Logan?"

The gesture was simple and wasn't in any way meant to be provocative. Hell, all she'd done was place her hand on his forearm, and that had been covered by his long-sleeved shirt. But the warmth from her touch, her soft voice saying his name just about turned him wrong side out.

Closing his eyes, he called himself nine kinds of a fool. But he was man enough to admit he was fighting a lost cause. "Do you know how to ride?"

She nodded, but there was indecision in her expression. "Sort of."

"What do you mean by that?" he asked.

"When I was a child, my parents used to have friends who owned a farm south of St. Louis. I sometimes rode their horse. But I think she was about a hundred years old."

"Horses don't live that long."

"You know what I mean." She gave him one of

those looks a woman always gives a man when she thinks he's being dense. "It was extremely old and didn't have a lot of energy left."

"In other words, you sat in the saddle and that's about it," he guessed.

"Correct."

Glancing down, he pointed to her feet. "Riding in tennis shoes isn't a good idea."

"Why?"

"There's no heel to keep your foot from slipping through the stirrup. If you fell off, you could be dragged or stepped on. Do you have a pair of boots?"

"Yes," she said, her eyes lighting with excitement. "Does this mean you'll take me with you?"

"Go put your boots on," he said, resigned. He decided it was almost worth the hell he'd go through for the next couple of days just to see the elation in her beautiful green eyes.

She reached up to give him a quick hug, sending his blood pressure up several notches and playing hell with his effort to get his body back under control. "Thank you, Logan."

When she turned and started jogging back to the house, he called after her. "Wear a long-sleeved shirt—preferably flannel—and a warm jacket."

"I'll be ready in twenty minutes," she said, disappearing into the house.

He sighed heavily and headed for the barn. He'd be a raving lunatic by the time they reached the campsite. How was he supposed to do any kind of soul-searching by taking the source of his torment with him? And how in hell was he going to keep his hands off her?

Several scenarios came to mind and made him so damned hard that riding a horse would undoubtedly prove hazardous. He rubbed a hand over his face in an effort to wipe out the erotic fantasies. It didn't help. He had the feeling he was fighting the inevitable.

After opening the stall of the oldest, gentlest horse he owned, he led Valentine to the door of the tack room. He quickly saddled the mare, led her out to where his gelding and the packhorse stood tied to the corral, then turned and headed for the house. He wasn't happy about what he was about to do, but a week ago he'd made Cassie a promise.

And although he didn't plan on kissing her, he'd be damned before he went back on his word.

Cassie glanced at Logan for at least the tenth time as they rode side by side across the valley toward the eastern mountains surrounding the Lazy Ace. She'd been so shocked by his appearance when he'd met her at the corral, she hadn't been able to ask how far they were going, how long it would take to get there or when they'd return.

One question kept running through her mind. Why had he shaved off his mustache?

He hadn't said more than a handful of words to her all morning, and if his unapproachable demeanor was any indication, he didn't want to talk about the absence of his facial hair. Or much of anything else, for that matter.

She knew he wasn't happy about her accompanying him up into the mountains, but that was too bad. For some reason it wasn't enough to hear about the land her uncle Silas had left her. She wanted to *see* it. Besides, what Hank had told her was true. It was dangerous for Logan to be traveling the mountains alone.

Closing her eyes, Cassie tilted her head back and breathed in the fresh, unpolluted air. The warmth of the sun on her upturned face felt wonderful. "Uncle Silas was right. This is the most beautiful place on earth."

"Really?" Logan didn't sound as if he believed her. "You like this better than the city?"

"Oh, yes. I wish I'd lived here when I was a child," she said, feeling more content than she had in years. "Bringing the girls out here to grow up is the best thing I've ever done. They'll always know this kind of beauty exists."

They rode in silence for several more minutes and had just ridden into the line of trees ringing the upland meadow when Logan asked, "What would your husband have thought of your decision to move the girls out here? Would he have approved of his daughters living somewhere out in the back forty of God's country?"

Cassie didn't particularly like discussing Stan, but she supposed Logan had a right to know, since she and the girls were here to stay. "Stan died in a car accident before the twins were born. But he wouldn't have cared one way or the other, even if he'd lived."

Logan reined in the gelding under a canopy of pine trees. "We'll eat lunch and rest the horses here," he said, waiting for her to stop the mare. Dismounting his horse, he helped her down from Valentine. "What do you mean, he wouldn't have cared?" he asked.

Shrugging, Cassie walked over to sit on a boulder at the base of a pine tree. "Stan didn't care for anyone or anything but himself. He'd filed for divorce two days before he was killed."

Logan opened one of the leather bags behind his saddle, then handed her a sandwich. Unwrapping his, he watched her take a bite. "So your husband never knew about Chelsea and Kelsie?"

Her appetite deserting her, she rewrapped her sandwich. "I didn't find out I was expecting twins until after he died. But he knew I was pregnant," she said, unable to keep the bitterness from her voice. "That's why he filed for divorce. He gave me a choice—I either terminated the pregnancy or he'd leave. I chose my babies."

Logan had leaned against a tree across from her and, although his stance appeared relaxed, she detected his tension in the tightening of his features. "What kind of man wants his wife to get rid of their child?" He sounded angry.

"A very selfish, self-centered one."

"Obviously." Logan shook his head. "So you've been on your own with the babies from the start."

She nodded. "And we're doing just fine. We have each other. We don't need a man in our lives."

Logan didn't comment further as he finished his lunch. He couldn't. He was still too outraged by what Cassie had told him. Her husband had to have been a class-A jerk—first for wanting her to get rid of their child and second for intending to leave her pregnant and alone.

Hadn't the man realized what he had? Stan Wellington had been gifted with everything Logan had ever wanted in life, but couldn't have—a wife and family. And in the process of throwing it all away, the man had convinced Cassie that she didn't want or need anyone to share her life, or to help her raise her daughters.

Maybe it was for the best that she and the twins had moved to the Lazy Ace, Logan decided. Living on a remote ranch with him was probably safer for the three of them than life alone in a big city. At least he'd be there to protect and take care of them for as long as they stayed.

He tried to extinguish the spark of hope building in his chest. Maybe they wouldn't leave. Maybe Cassie and the twins would stay and allow him to feel as if he were a part of their family from time to time.

Yeah, and cattle roost in trees.

Stretching, Logan walked over to where he'd ground-tied the horses and picked up the reins of the gelding and mare. "We'd better get moving if we want to make camp by supper."

Cassie nodded and walked over to Valentine. "Why do my legs feel like limp spaghetti?"

Logan smiled. "You're not used to riding."

He put his hands around her trim waist and prepared to help her mount up. Touching her in any way played hell with his libido, but when he helped lift her into the saddle, her cute little rear bobbing in front of his face had him biting back a groan.

Swinging up onto his horse, he ground his teeth

against the pure and utter frustration gnawing at his gut. If he had any sense, he'd turn them around and head back to the ranch. If the simple act of helping her onto a horse had his blood flowing like fire through his veins, there was no way in hell he'd be able to keep his hands to himself lying beside her tonight in that tiny little tent.

By midafternoon the trail had narrowed and they were forced to ride single file. Logan frequently twisted in his saddle to look back at Cassie. He wanted to make sure she wasn't having any problems keeping up with him.

"Doing okay?"

She smiled. "Just fine."

"Good. We still have a few more miles to go before we make camp."

The trail forked a few yards ahead, and he'd just started to guide Dakota up the right path when the guttural grunt of a bear combined with Cassie's piercing scream made Logan's hair stand on end and set Dakota to crow hopping. He immediately got the gelding calmed, but the rope he'd used to tie the packhorse to the back of his saddle snapped. He watched a few of their supplies go flying through the air as old Smokey bucked like a rank bronc in a two-bit rodeo, then broke into a dead run as he headed back down the mountain, taking the rest of their camping gear with him.

And Cassie had raised such a ruckus she'd scared poor old Samson right out of his hide. Bellowing and crashing through the brush like a steamroller, the bear was putting as much distance as he could between himself and the unhinged female who'd screamed bloody murder. Logan figured the bear would be half-way around the mountain before he finally stopped.

Fortunately, Valentine had a calm enough nature she hadn't started bucking, but her ears were pinned back and her nostrils flared wide. Logan wasn't sure which one was showing more of the whites of their eyes, the woman or the mare. But he did know beyond a shadow of doubt that if Cassie didn't stop squirming around in the saddle, the frightened mare would wind up following the packhorse down the mountain and take Cassie with her.

Quickly grabbing the mare's reins to keep her from fleeing, he tried to soothe both the woman and the horse. "Easy now, sugar. He's gone."

"Are you sure?" Cassie asked anxiously, still twisting around to see which direction Samson had fled. Logan had to get her to calm down.

Bringing Valentine alongside his horse, Logan didn't hesitate. He held both sets of reins in one hand, then wrapped his other arm around Cassie's waist and hauled her onto his lap. The gelding shied at the extra weight, but Logan managed to hold both horses, the woman and his temper. Barely.

Their camping supplies were halfway down the mountain and he'd probably never see his bear again.

But when Cassie put both arms around his neck and clung to him as tremors racked her slender body, his anger melted like an ice cube on a hot plate. She was seated across his lap, so her warm little bottom pressing against his groin and her breasts crushed to his chest had the predictable effect. He bit back a groan. He was hotter than hell and there was no way he'd be able to hide it when she calmed down.

But that was the least of his worries at the moment. The packhorse had dislodged several items as it pitched and ran down the mountain. He needed to get down and assess what they had left of their supplies and what they were missing.

He quickly judged the distance they'd traveled. They were too far from the house to make it home by dark. Win, lose, or draw, they were going to have to spend the night on the mountain with a minimal amount of camping gear.

Cassie watched Logan squat and sort through what remained of their supplies. He didn't look happy.

"Is that all we have left?" she asked cautiously.

Nodding, he rose to his feet. "We have a granite coffeepot, but no coffee, some jerky and a couple of candy bars in my saddlebags, one sleeping bag and no tent."

"Will we be able to make it back to the house before dark?" She had a sinking feeling she already knew the answer, but decided to ask anyway.

"No."

His clipped answer made her feel worse. "Look, I said I'm sorry."

"Tell that to Samson."

She walked over to him and, propping her hands on her hips, glared up at him. "How was I to know that stupid bear was the one you raised from a cub? To me, one bear looks just like any other—hairy, with big claws and a lot of teeth. And for your information, Mr. Logan Murdock, where I come from, they're all considered wild and *very* dangerous."

"Samson isn't," he said stubbornly.

"Well, if I ever meet up with Samson again, I'll try to keep that in mind and give my best effort to containing myself." She walked over to sit on a fallen tree trunk, propped her elbow on her knee and rested her cheek in her hand. "Just tell me what we have to do to get through the night."

"You're going to sit tight while I go find some wood to build a fire." He started to stalk off into the forest, but turned back. "And do me a favor, will you?"

"What's that?"

"Try not to send any more of the wildlife running for their lives."

She knew it was childish and she would never tolerate it from the twins when they got older, but she couldn't stop herself. She made a face and stuck her tongue out at his retreating back.

As she sat there waiting for Logan to return to the edge of the little clearing, she looked around at the mixture of pine and aspen trees, watched a rabbit nibble on grass and heard an eagle's shrill cry as it circled somewhere in the sky above. The rabbit scurried for cover at the sound and she realized that even though it was the most breathtaking place she'd ever been, it was still a harsh environment where the law of survival still reigned supreme.

Maybe that's what appealed to her about the area. She liked the idea of her daughters growing up knowing that, although the scenery was unquestionably beautiful, the land commanded respect and discipline. Here they would learn to become strong, capable women who appreciated the beauty of life as well as respecting its harshness. Just as she was doing.

Lost in thought, she jumped when Logan strolled back into the clearing, his arms loaded with wood for the fire. He arched a brow, but apparently knew better than to mention her frightened movement. Either that, or the glare she sent his way had worked, because he wisely let the moment pass without comment.

"Did you see any signs of the packhorse?" she asked hopefully. She really felt guilty about frightening the poor animal.

Logan shook his head. "Smokey's traveled these mountains enough with me that he knows his way around. We'll find him grazing somewhere down in the meadow on the way home tomorrow."

"He'll be all right?" She wanted to make sure the horse would come to no harm.

"Should be," Logan said, nodding. He arranged sticks and dried leaves around the stack of small logs he'd laid for their campfire.

"Why do we need a fire if there's nothing to cook?"

When he looked up, his expression held a mixture of amusement and exasperation. "Three reasons. First, since the lanterns went down the trail with Smokey, I didn't figure you'd want to stumble around in the dark. Second, it should keep the wildlife away so you don't scare the hell out of them. And third, I'm not in favor of freezing our asses off tonight when the temperature dips down in the low thirties. Any more questions?"

"No."

He took a small box of matches from his vest pocket and in no time had a nice fire blazing. Rising, he picked up the coffeepot. "There's a spring about a hundred yards from here. I'll be back in a few minutes with water."

Cassie nodded, then watched Logan until he disappeared among the trees. He had to have the widest shoulders and sexiest rump of any cowboy in Wyoming.

Honed by years of physical labor, the man's body was absolutely gorgeous. Remembering the feel of his warm skin and his hard muscles pressed to her the night they'd fallen on the bed made her cheeks warm and her stomach flutter. When he'd kissed her, his mustache had grazed her lips, her throat, her breasts and heightened her passion until she'd lost every ounce of common sense she possessed.

What would it be like for him to kiss her now that he'd shaved? He'd said he wouldn't kiss her again. Did he mean it?

A part of her wanted him to take her into his arms and make her feel the way she had the other times he'd kissed her. But another part of her wanted him to stay as far away as possible.

Both times he'd held her, touched his firm lips to hers and explored her with his tongue, she'd lost all control and given in to a need that was unlike anything she'd ever felt before. It was as if he'd awakened something deep inside her that she hadn't known existed. Something that both excited her and at the same time scared her to death.

What would it be like to make love to Logan? To see all of his magnificent body? To feel it touch every part of her? To have his strength buried deep inside her body as he held her close?

A wave of longing coursed through Cassie, making her shiver. Suddenly too restless to sit, she stood and began pacing. But the movement did little to divert her overactive mind. Why hadn't she thought things through, instead of insisting that he bring her along on his trip? Why couldn't she have waited to see the rest of what she'd inherited until someone else could come along with them?

Several facts seemed to invade her brain at once—details that she definitely should have considered before they left the Lazy Ace. They were up in the mountains, miles away from another living soul. They were spending the night together. And they might…

She gritted her teeth and closed her eyes. "Don't think about it."

Logan stared across the campfire at Cassie. What the hell was wrong with her? When he'd returned with the water she'd been walking the perimeter of the clearing like a caged animal. But as soon as she'd seen him, she'd hurried over to the fallen tree, plopped down and avoided looking at him. And she wasn't talking much, either.

He'd tried several times to draw her into a conversation, but hadn't gotten more than one or two words out of her. And most of those had been "no."

Removing his Resistol, he scratched his head. She

wasn't thirsty. She wasn't cold. And she wasn't hungry. What the hell was left?

She put her delicate hand up to her mouth to hide a huge yawn. Of course. That had to be it. She had to be bone tired. They'd left the house around six that morning, ridden all day and it was well past ten now.

"Would you like for me to get the sleeping bag spread out for you?" he asked, rising to his feet.

She looked at him then. "Where are you sleeping?"

So that was it. She was having reservations about their sleeping arrangements. Well, that made two of them. It was bothering the hell out of him, too.

"I'm staying up for another couple of hours," he said, stretching and rotating his shoulders. "I want to keep the fire going a while longer."

"Oh." She looked thoughtful. "Our jackets were on the packhorse. Will you be warm enough?"

He almost laughed. Almost.

Instead, he shrugged and tried for a nonchalant expression. There was no way in hell he could tell her that after watching her all evening and seeing the light from the fire play across her beautiful features, thinking about lying next to her in that sleeping bag had him hotter than a prize bull in a herd of eager heifers. Nor could he tell her that when he did turn in for the night, he was going to have to crawl into the bag with her or risk freezing off vital parts of his anatomy.

"I'll be fine," he said, picking up the thick insulated roll. He checked to make sure the area was clear of rocks and sticks, then spread out the bedding, unzipped the side and stepped back. "It's ready any time you are."

When she just stood there looking at him, Logan shifted from one foot to the other. Was there something else she wanted him to do?

"What?" he asked.

"Turn your head. I want to take my jeans off."

At her announcement, the flame in the pit of his belly flared up and his instantaneous arousal pushed against his jeans. He hadn't even given thought to the fact that they'd be taking off their clothing.

But Cassie wasn't thinking about that. She was just trying to get comfortable. She didn't realize that she wouldn't be spending the night in there by herself. But he did.

"Well?"

Nodding, he quickly spun around and walked to the other side of the campfire. He tried not to think as he stood there staring into the darkness, trying to force air into his lungs. But his memory was far too good.

He'd seen her luscious body on two separate occasions—the night they'd fallen on her bed and the afternoon she'd come down with the flu. Remembering the sight of her perfect breasts and her moans of pleasure when he'd taken her into his mouth made his jeans damned uncomfortable and his breathing problems worse.

When he heard the sound of the zipper sliding up on the sleeping bag, he took a deep breath and turned around. Good. Cassie was lying on her side, facing the other way.

Right then and there, Logan made a decision. Unless it got colder than a well digger's ass in January, he was staying out of that sleeping bag.

Eight

Hours later and colder than he'd been in years, Logan shrugged out of his vest, pulled off his boots and shucked his jeans. Shivering, he unzipped the side of the sleeping bag. He'd been fine for a while, but as the temperature dropped to the low thirties and a slight breeze blew down the mountain from the snow-capped peaks at the higher elevations, he'd damned near frozen his tail off. Among other things.

Doing his best not to wake Cassie, he nudged her over a bit, then shimmied into the insulated bedding. He quickly zipped the side, then lay there shivering. He could feel her warmth pressed to his side. He would not turn to her for warmth. He wouldn't.

His teeth chattering, he finally gave up, turned over and spooned her. Her warm little body felt good as he snuggled against her back, and some of the chill that had seeped into him began to recede.

He tried to ignore the smell of baby powder and sweet, warm woman. Why he found the combination so damned erotic, he didn't even want to try analyzing. Some shrink would probably interpret it as being a subconscious desire to procreate with Cassie. The thought lit a spark of warmth somewhere deep inside him and began to spread to his lower regions.

Tilting his head back as far as he could, he tried his best to escape the intoxicating scent. He figured the way his luck had been running lately, a storm would probably come up, it would start raining and he'd drown. He almost laughed. Drowning would be preferable to having Cassie wake up and find him in an undeniable state of readiness.

When she moved in her sleep and wiggled her bottom against his groin, Logan closed his eyes and gritted his teeth. He had to keep his mind off the fact that the only thing separating him from paradise were two scraps of cotton—his briefs and her panties.

He mentally ran through the list of things he and Hank still needed to repair on the foreman's cabin. It didn't help.

He tried easing himself away from her, but damned if she didn't follow. His lower body tightened and expanded.

Taking a deep breath, he mentally ran through every batting average of every baseball player he'd ever heard of. When that didn't work, he held his breath and tried willing away his arousal. There wasn't enough blood left in his brain to concentrate on anything but the feel of Cassie's cute little bottom pressed against the part of him that wanted her to be there the most.

She sighed and murmured his name in her sleep. He came to full erection. His eyes popped open and, looking skyward, he prayed for divine intervention.

Cassie turned in his arms to face him, her legs tangling with his. He stifled the groan that had been building from the moment he crawled into the sleeping bag. But when she draped her arm over him and burrowed closer, the softness of her breasts indicated that she'd taken off her bra before crawling into the sleeping bag. He couldn't stop it. The sound came rumbling out of him and he automatically tightened his arms around her.

He watched her lashes flutter, slowly start to lift, then snap wide open. Before she could start the tirade he knew was inevitable, he shook his head. "Don't say a word. Just turn back over and stop your damned squirming."

He might have known she'd ignore what he'd told her.

"I thought you said you were staying up?" It sounded more like an accusation than a question.

"I got cold," he said through clenched teeth. "Now, turn over and go back to sleep."

"I can't."

His face so close to hers he could see tiny flecks of brown in her green eyes, he glared at her. "Why not?"

She stared back at him. "I can't move."

"Why?"

"You're holding me."

Instantly loosening his arms, he waited for her to move. She didn't. She just lay there gazing at him. "Dammit, Cassie, it's taking everything I've got to be a gentleman. Now, roll over, or I swear I won't be responsible for what happens.''

Her eyes wide, she turned over and he breathed a sigh of relief. It was short-lived.

"Logan?"

It would be a lot easier on him if she'd just go to sleep. The sound of her voice saying his name was playing hell with his good intentions.

"What?"

"Could I ask you something?"

He sighed heavily. "What do you want to know, Cassie?"

"Tell me why you shaved your mustache."

"It's not important." How could he tell her that, although he wasn't planning on kissing her, he'd shaved just in case, so she wouldn't get any more whisker burns?

"The twins are going to be disappointed."

He knew he shouldn't ask. The sound of her soft voice was driving his libido into overdrive. But instead of letting the matter drop, he allowed curiosity to get the better of him. He didn't like the idea of Cassie or her babies being disappointed in him in any way.

"Why do you think that?" he asked.

"They liked the feel of your mustache. It tickled their hands and made them laugh."

Her soft voice, the scent of her and the warmth of her body so close to his own were playing havoc with his good intentions. He wondered what Cassie thought.

"What about you? Will you miss my mustache?" He couldn't believe he'd asked what had been running through his mind.

Her hip brushed his erection as she turned over to face him, and Logan sucked in a sharp breath. But when she brought her hand up to touch his upper lip with her finger, he closed his eyes and tried to remember all the reasons he couldn't make love to her. He couldn't think of a damned one.

"Yes." She looked thoughtful. "I think I will miss it. It was soft and made my lips tingle."

He'd given being a gentleman a damned good shot, but Cassie wasn't cooperating and he was tired of trying. Catching her finger in his, he brought it to his mouth and kissed the tip. "But don't you remember the promise I made you about a week ago?"

She looked confused. "That you wouldn't kiss me?"

Logan smiled and shook his head. "No, sugar. I never said I wouldn't kiss you again. I gave you my word that I'd never leave a mark on you."

She continued to stare at him and Logan watched desire begin to darken her eyes. "So you shaved because you intended to kiss me while we're up here in the mountains?" she asked, her soft voice sending a ripple of longing straight to his core.

"Not exactly, sugar." He chuckled. "I shaved because I didn't want to run the risk of breaking my promise in case we did kiss."

"Oh." She looked thoughtful for several long moments, then, smiling, asked, "Would you kiss me so I could see what it feels like without your mustache?"

He stopped breathing and couldn't have forced the air out of his lungs if his life depended on it. When he finally got his voice to work, he shook his head.

"Sugar, don't get me wrong. There's nothing I'd like to do more than to kiss you until we're both senseless. But all things considered, it wouldn't be a good idea. I don't think I could stop with just a kiss."

"You're probably right." She smiled. "I doubt that I'd be able to stop, either."

With her simple admission, his heart felt as if it slammed into his rib cage, then took off at breakneck speed. Was she telling him she wanted to make love with him?

"Cassie?"

From the light of the campfire, he could see her close her eyes for a moment, then open them. Her gaze met his, steady and sure. "Yes."

All the fight went out of him and he pulled her close. Burying his face in the red-gold cloud of her hair, he asked, "Sugar, are you sure this is what you want?"

She nodded.

Taking a deep breath, he struggled with what needed to be said. She was a nester, and no matter how much he'd like things to be different, he couldn't in good conscience offer her any kind of commitment.

"Cassie, I'm not making any promises."

"I know," she said softly. "I'm not asking for any."

He pressed his lips to her forehead and held her close. As much as he would hurt physically, he'd rather endure whatever hell he had to go through than have her regret one second of making love with him. "I don't want you having any regrets."

"None." The sureness he detected in her voice

convinced him she meant what she'd said. Her hands unsnapping his shirt put that certainty into action.

Spreading the chambray back, she placed her soft hands on his chest and stroked his skin with her fingertips. "You're beautiful."

He chuckled. "Sugar, I've been called a lot of things in my time, but beautiful never has been one of them."

She smiled. "It should be. Your body is perfect."

"Not as perfect as yours," he said, lowering his mouth to hers.

Cassie's eyes drifted shut at the contact of Logan's lips on hers, and a surge of longing stronger than anything she'd ever experienced coursed through her. When he slipped his tongue inside to stroke, tease and entice hers, her heart skipped a beat and her body tingled all over.

He continued to explore her with his mouth as he eased her onto her back. Pillowing her head on his forearm, he threaded his fingers through her hair and ran his other hand along her side, down to her hip, then smoothed it over her bare thigh. Every nerve in her body sizzled to life and shivers of excitement ran through her at the feel of his callused palm tenderly chafing her sensitized skin.

Logan brought his hand up to her stomach and released the button at the bottom of her flannel shirt. Slowly, surely, he pushed each small disk through its opening, then brushed the garment aside. Cupping her breast, he broke the kiss to nibble his way to the hollow at the base of her throat. His tongue darted out to touch the rapid fluttering there, then he nipped and kissed his way down the slope of her breast to the sensitive tip.

He raised his head to look down at her, and the desire she saw in the depths of his navy gaze stole her breath. His smile reassuring, he lowered his lips to her nipple. The feel of Logan taking her into his mouth, his gentle suckling of her puckered flesh caused her blood to thicken and course through her like warm honey. At her moan of pleasure, he increased his demands and an empty ache began to build deep inside her.

She held his head to her and reveled in the hot sensations flowing to every cell in her body. He trailed his hand down her abdomen and she raised her hips as he pushed her panties out of the way. Touching her gently, he parted her legs, and the coil inside of her tightened to deep need. Stroking and teasing, demanding and coaxing, he created a firestorm within her, and she thought she'd die from the passion racing through her. Never had her excitement been higher, the heat within her more intense, than it was at that very moment. Never had she wanted a man as much as she wanted Logan.

But just when she thought she'd die from the intensity of her need, he lifted his head to smile down at her. Catching her hand in his, he guided her to the hard ridge of his arousal, straining at his cotton briefs.

"I want you to touch me, Cassie. I want you to feel how much I want to make you mine."

His deep baritone, roughened by the strain of unfulfilled desire, flowed over her, and as she touched him, Cassie felt him surge beneath the cotton. It wasn't enough. She wanted to feel his taut skin, the velvet warmth of him. She wanted to bring him the same pleasure he was giving her.

With his help, she shoved his briefs down his thighs and caught the length of him in her trembling hands. Encased in the sleeping bag as they were, she couldn't see him, but closing her eyes she memorized his length with her fingers, his strength with her palms.

His groan of pleasure encouraged her, and she boldly stroked him until his big body shuddered from the strain of barely leashed desire.

"Open your eyes, sugar," Logan said through gritted teeth. "Look at me."

Doing as he commanded, she felt her heart race when her gaze met his. She'd never had a man look at her that way. Logan was laying his soul bare, allowing her to see the storm raging within him, showing her how deeply his hunger for her ran.

He held her captive with his eyes, and their gazes locked as they explored each other with their hands. Cassie thought she'd die from the empty ache Logan had created, but the intense passion she watched build in his deep blue eyes told her that he was feeling the need just as deeply as she was.

"Please, Logan. Make love to me now."

She watched a troubled look suddenly replace the passion on his face. Stopping the sensual torment, he closed his eyes, took her hands in his and clutched them to his chest. He leaned his forehead on hers and took a deep breath, then another.

"I'd rather die than say this, but...I can't make

love to you, sugar. I didn't plan on this happening and I don't have anything to protect you.''

If they stopped now, she knew for certain that she'd die from wanting. She quickly did a mental calculation and thanked the heavens above that she'd always been as regular as clockwork. "I don't think we have anything to worry about. It should be a safe time.''

"Are you sure?''

"Yes.''

He groaned and wrapped her in his arms. "You don't know how glad I am to hear you say that.''

Cassie would have told him how much she agreed, but at the moment she couldn't. The feel of his big body against her chased away all thought and left her with nothing but the ability to feel.

She'd never in her life pleaded with a man to make love to her, never believed she ever would. But in Logan's arms she was doing a lot of things she'd never done before. "Logan, please make love to me.''

Without a word, he kissed her with such mind-shattering tenderness it brought tears to her eyes. Moving restlessly against him, she found him with her hands and once again marveled at the power of his arousal, his need for her.

He slipped his hand between them to chafe the nub of her passion, then slipped his finger inside to stroke her to frenzied readiness. She felt as if she'd go up in flames at any moment.

"Logan...please.''

"Easy, sugar,'' he said, nudging her legs farther apart with his knee.

Levering himself over her, he found her with the tip of his arousal and, taking a deep breath, slowly, gently began to push his hips forward. His size, the sheer power of his body as he entered her was overwhelming, and she was reminded just how long it had been since she'd made love with a man.

Once his body was completely joined with hers, he braced himself on his elbows and looked down at her. The light from the dying campfire made the sweat beading his forehead and upper lip glisten and she could tell by the slight trembling of his taut muscles just how much his restraint was costing him. But he remained perfectly still as he gave her time to adjust. Her heart swelled at his consideration, his desire to make her feel safe with him.

"It's been a while for you, hasn't it?" he asked, smiling down at her.

She'd never felt more cherished, more desired. She wished she could tell him how special he made her feel, but she couldn't get words past the huge lump clogging her throat.

Brushing a strand of hair from her cheek, he gave her a tender smile. "Take a deep breath and relax, sugar. I'm going to make sure there's nothing but pleasure for you."

He lowered his lips to hers, and his kiss set off sparklers behind her closed eyelids. Slowly pulling back, he eased his hips forward, then repeated the process, increasing his pace as she responded by arching into his thrusts. Desire suddenly gave way to powerful need and Cassie felt herself racing toward fulfillment.

Her heart skipped several beats when she realized

that Logan was taking her to a place she'd never been, drawing responses from her only he could elicit. Together they were creating a realm for just the two of them, a place where their souls would unite.

The thought frightened her, but as the pleasure built and her body tightened, she refused to analyze what it all meant. All she could do was feel.

Suddenly wave after wave of shattering sensation crashed over her and she felt Logan's body stiffen, then surge into her one last time as he filled her with his essence.

Logan slowly became aware of his surroundings. Realizing his weight had to be crushing Cassie, he eased himself to her side, then gathered her to him. "Are you all right?"

"Yes."

When she burrowed deeper into his arms, Logan kissed the top of her head. "I know it's been a long time. I didn't hurt you, did I?"

She shook her head, then in a quiet voice added, "Thank you."

He knew a moment of fear. She was thanking him? For what? For not hurting her? Had her husband been rough with her? The thought twisted Logan's gut and made him want to sink his fist into the bastard's nose.

Tightening his arms around her, Logan asked, "What for, sugar?"

Her soft laughter eased his tension. "I've never felt anything like what we just shared," she said, her lips brushing his throat as she spoke. He wouldn't have believed it possible this soon, but his body was beginning to respond again to the feel of her sweet mouth whispering against his skin. "Thank you for that," she finished.

"You mean you've never climaxed before?" he asked incredulously.

"Well, I have," she admitted. She giggled self-consciously. "But it was nothing like that. That was incredible. I never knew foreplay could last that long, or be that intense."

Logan's chest tightened with satisfaction and a healthy dose of male pride. The way he saw it, he was the one who should be thanking her. Didn't she realize what it meant to a man to have a woman admit he was the best she'd ever had?

Possessiveness—so strong it damned near shut off his breathing—tightened his chest and closed around his throat. The thought scared the hell out of him, but there was no use denying it. He never wanted her feeling that way about anyone else. Just him.

His body hardened with a primitive desire to show her once again that she belonged to him. Shifting her to lie on top of him, Logan allowed her to feel the evidence of his need. He watched surprise turn to passion in the depths of her expressive green eyes, and satisfaction filled his soul.

Logan lay awake long after Cassie had drifted off into an exhausted sleep. Gazing at the millions of stars overhead, he tried to come to grips with what he was feeling and how radically his perspective had changed.

He and Cassie had made love twice, and instead of satisfying the craving he'd had since the moment he laid eyes on her, it had only served to whet his appetite. As incredible as it seemed, he wanted her yet again.

Something deep inside told him he always would.

He pressed a kiss to the top of her head and held her close as he stared off into the vastness of the wide Wyoming sky. Two weeks ago he couldn't come up with enough reasons to convince Cassie to leave the Lazy Ace. Now he couldn't think of enough ways to make sure she stayed.

Maybe he'd been wrong. Maybe she wouldn't leave.

She genuinely seemed to love the land as much as he did, and he found that he wanted to share more of it with her. The next camping trip they took, he'd show her Shadow Valley, where the elk and mule deer grazed in huge numbers and a waterfall cascaded to the valley floor below. And, if she was still on the ranch in the spring, he'd take her to the higher elevations, where they could watch the eagles feeding their young.

The dangers of being in such an isolated area still caused a pang of uneasiness deep within him, but Logan acknowledged it, then put it aside. Hank was right. People in town got sick and died the same as people in remote regions. He'd just have to be extra vigilant about keeping Cassie and the twins healthy and safe.

Determination filled Logan's soul. He'd succeed in the one area where his father had failed.

Forced to ride single file down the mountain trail, Cassie watched Logan turn in his saddle to look back at her. "You doing okay?"

"Valentine and I are just fine," she said. Smiling, she patted the mare's neck. "We're enjoying all this beautiful scenery."

When he turned back toward the trail, she stared at his broad shoulders and decided the scenery was more than wonderful—it was downright devastating. She'd been right about him. He was a sorcerer. With one simple kiss he could make her body hum and stars twinkle behind her closed eyes.

What they'd shared last night certainly hadn't been planned. Far from it. But making love with Logan had been one of the most incredible experiences of her life.

She should have known it would be that way. From the moment they met, the sexual tension arcing between them had been a tangible thing, and although they'd both fought its pull, they hadn't been able to resist.

Deep in her heart, Cassie knew that neither of them had been given a choice in the matter. It had been their fate.

She sighed. Heaven only knew she wasn't comfortable with it, but if she wasn't in love with Logan yet, she didn't have far to go to get there. And it frightened her more than any predator ever could. She didn't need a man complicating her life.

Maybe it would be best for all concerned if she reconsidered her decision to live on the Lazy Ace, took the twins and returned to St. Louis. It might be the only thing that would save her from having her heart completely shattered.

If she was in love with Logan, would he ever love her in return?

And what about the twins? Would he be able to love them, as well?

Stan hadn't been at all happy about the prospect of being a father, even though the girls were a part of him—his own flesh and blood. Of course, if he'd lived he might have had a change of heart once they were born, but that was highly doubtful. He'd simply been too shallow and self-centered to care for anyone or anything but himself.

Was Logan like that?

Cassie didn't think so. When she'd been ill, he'd taken time away from running the ranch to care for the girls, and had even seemed to enjoy the task. But baby-sitting was different than being a full-time parent.

And some men didn't like the idea of a ready-made family.

Could Logan accept another man's children as his own? He'd told her point-blank he never intended to have children of his own, so he certainly wouldn't want someone else's. Would he?

Nine

Logan crossed his arms over his chest and leaned his shoulder against the door frame as he watched Cassie slowly move around the kitchen. She had to be bone tired.

They'd ridden for two solid days and spent all of last night making love instead of sleeping. Then after they'd returned to the house late this afternoon, Hank and Ginny had left for a few days down in Laramie to see Hank's grandmother. Logan had offered to help Cassie with the babies, but, saying she wanted to spend time with them, she'd fed and bathed them herself.

He'd felt a little left out, but he had also understood her need for a little space. Things had changed between them, and no matter where they ended up, they both knew there was no turning back.

Walking over to her, Logan took the plate she held and put it in the dishwasher, then turned to take her into his arms. "You're dead on your feet. Why don't you go on upstairs to bed, sugar?"

"I still have to finish loading the dishwasher and…" She yawned. "I have to do a load of laundry."

He shook his head. "I'll finish the dishes and start the clothes." Holding her soft body to his was heaven and hell rolled into one. He wanted her with a fierceness that damned near brought him to his knees, but she needed rest. "Go on and get some sleep."

She leaned up, kissed his chin, then stepped out of his embrace. "Thank you," she said before walking down the hall to the stairs.

It took everything Logan had to keep from following her, hauling her luscious body back into his arms and kissing her until they both gasped for air. But she needed rest, and he knew for certain that if he gave in to the urge to kiss her, they'd end up missing another night's sleep.

After making quick work of loading the dishwasher, he started the washing machine. Now what? he wondered as he wandered into the living room.

He stared at the couch, then at the big comfortable armchair with the ottoman. If he wasn't afraid of wrinkling the slipcovers, he'd sit down and watch a little television. He still wasn't wild about the changes in decor, but he didn't want to mess anything up, either. Cassie had worked hard on the room and she was proud of the way it looked.

He shook his head. When had he accepted the changes she'd made?

He chuckled. She'd stormed into his life, turned his world upside down and all he could think of was how amazing she was. She'd made his house a home, and until he'd taken care of Kelsie and Chelsea, he'd never considered how hard Cassie worked to keep a clean house and care for two tiny little girls at the same time. And even though she made it look easy, he didn't want to create more work for her.

While he stood there trying to decide what to do, Logan heard one of the babies cry. Not wanting Cassie to be disturbed, he took the stairs two at a time and opened the door to the twins' room.

As soon as the baby saw him, she cried harder and raised her little arms for him to pick her up. His heart melted right then and there.

Lifting the copper-haired little girl to his chest, he asked, ''What's wrong, little one? Did you have a bad dream?''

She wrapped her chubby little arms around his neck and sobbed. What little remained of the wall he'd had around his heart for so many years fell into a pile of dust. He was a goner.

Logan checked on Chelsea to make sure she hadn't been disturbed by Kelsie's cries, then took the baby downstairs with him.

The baby continued to whimper and chew on her fist while he paced around the living room, wondering if he should wake Cassie. He'd checked, and Kelsie's diaper was clean and dry.

Fear suddenly gnawed at his gut. Was the baby sick? Did she need to see a doctor?

Just when he'd decided he'd better wake Cassie, the baby quieted down, stuck her thumb into her mouth and laid her head on his shoulder. He hugged the tiny girl close and hummed tunelessly.

When had he changed his mind about not wanting kids around? Hell, he'd walk through hellfire and damnation for the twins. Not to mention doing the same thing for their mother.

What would he do if Cassie and the twins left the Lazy Ace now? Would he be able to go back to the way things had been, as if they'd never invaded his home? His life?

Logan sat down in the armchair with the baby curled up on his chest and rubbed her little back. Closing his eyes, he asked himself the same question time and again. Could he go on living without them?

He didn't think so. They'd moved in, created total chaos in his blissful bachelor existence and filled a void in his life that he hadn't known existed.

Cassie yawned and stretched as she started downstairs to cook breakfast. She still wasn't fully rested from the camping trip, but at least she didn't feel as much like a zombie as she had last night.

At the bottom of the steps she glanced toward the living room and stopped short. Sound asleep, Logan was sprawled out in the armchair, his feet propped on the ottoman and one of the twins curled up comfortably on his wide chest. The sight was so touching it brought tears to her eyes.

She stood staring at the big man holding her daughter so tenderly. Now she knew for certain that Logan was nothing like Stan.

Apparently Kelsie had been restless last night and, instead of waking Cassie, he'd taken care of the baby himself. Stan would never have done anything like that. Stan had been self-centered and *never* did anything for anyone, unless it could benefit him in some way.

Logan, on the other hand, was selfless and took care of everyone around him.

Oh, he tried to bluff his way into making everyone think he was some type of self-contained, cowboy loner. But she'd experienced, firsthand, his caring nature when she'd had the flu. And what man, other than a father, would walk the floor with a fussy baby rather than wake the mother to take over?

Logan had known just how exhausted she'd been last night, and he'd insisted on finishing up her evening chores so she could get some rest. He'd also taken care of Kelsie as if she were his own child.

Tears filled her eyes. He tried to hide behind a tough exterior, but inside he was a marshmallow with more love to give than anyone she'd ever known.

Wiping the moisture that had escaped down her cheeks, she eased her sleeping daughter out of his arms and climbed the stairs to put Kelsie back in her crib. Cassie wasn't exactly sure when it had happened, but there was no sense in trying to deny it any longer.

She'd fallen head over heels in love with Logan Murdock.

Logan awoke with the distinct feeling that something wasn't quite right. Slowly opening his eyes, he stretched his arms, then scratched his chest.

Fear like nothing he'd ever known suddenly twisted his gut and choked off his air supply.

"Oh, damn!"

Jumping to his feet, he searched the chair for Kelsie. Where the hell was the baby? What had he done with her? Dear God, if anything happened to her, he'd never forgive himself.

He checked around the chair. Nothing. He threw the ruffled pillows from the couch to the floor. He got down on his hands and knees and crawled around looking under end tables and behind chairs. No baby.

Scared spitless, he felt his hands shake as he ran both of them through his hair. He'd vowed to protect them, to keep them all safe. How could he let something like this happen?

Think, Murdock.

The last thing he remembered before drifting off to sleep, he'd placed the baby on her stomach in the middle of his chest and started rubbing her back with his hand. She'd fussed a little, but then settled down and...and...

"What on earth are you doing?" Cassie asked from the stairs.

Logan turned to face her. How in hell was he going to tell her he'd lost her daughter?

"Cassie, I don't want you to get upset. We'll find her," he blurted.

"Find who?"

"Kelsie," he said, glancing around the living room again. Where could one little girl, who couldn't do anything more than crawl, have gone?

"She was restless last night and I didn't want to

wake you. So I brought her down here," he explained

"That sometimes happens with teething babies," she agreed.

"Right. Anyway, I walked the floor with her for a while." He glanced around the room again, hoping to see the little girl. "Then I sat down in the chair with her and we both fell asleep. When I woke up just now she was gone."

"Oh, I'm sure she'll turn up somewhere," Cassie said, grinning.

When she turned to walk down the hall to the kitchen, Logan reached out, placed both of his hands on her shoulders and spun her around. "You know damned good and well where Kelsie is, don't you?"

Cassie laughed. "Yes. She's in her crib."

"And just how the hell did she get there?" he demanded, his relief giving way to irritation.

"I took her upstairs and put her back to bed." Cassie put her arms around his waist and gazed up at him. "I came downstairs to start breakfast and found the two of you sound asleep in the chair." She grinned, her eyes twinkling merrily. "You know, you're really cute without your hat."

"Am not."

"Are too." She traced her finger across his brow, and his insides caught fire. "Now stop frowning. It makes you look cranky."

"That's because I'm peeved," he said, trying not to smile. She'd flashed her killer dimples at him and his anger had melted away like snow on a hot July day. He caught her hand in his and brought it to his lips. Kissing the finger she'd used to smooth his brow, he warned, "You're not getting out of this that easy, sugar. I was scared to death that something had happened to Kelsie."

"She's fine."

"But I didn't know that," he said, taking her fingertip into his mouth. Gently sucking on it, he added, "You owe me."

"For…what?" To his satisfaction, she sounded breathless.

"You made me worry for no reason." He leaned down to rest his forehead on hers. "That calls for retribution."

Her eyes darkened to forest green as she stared up at him. "What did you have in mind?"

"Definitely something that will teach you a lesson." His body tightened as it always did when he held her. "Something you'll remember for quite a while."

"Sounds interesting."

"It will be." He reached down to place both of his hands on her jeans-clad rear and pulled her close. Pressing his arousal to her lower belly, he finished, "But it's a lesson that has to be repeated periodically so you won't forget."

"I do seem to have a *very* short memory." The look she gave him made his body harden. "Is this something you've taught me before?" she asked.

Logan nodded and kissed her until they were both breathless. Grinning, he promised, "Only this time it's going to be a longer, better lesson."

"Better?" She looked surprised.

"Oh, yeah. This time our movements won't be confined by the sleeping bag. And we'll be able to see what we're doing." He tucked her to his side and headed upstairs. As they passed the twins' room, he was careful to keep his voice low. "How long before they wake up?"

"Another couple of hours." She grinned at him and the desire in her eyes sent a searing heat straight to his groin.

"Good." He quickly opened the door to his room, then ushered Cassie inside. Cupping her face between his palms, he smiled down at her. "I was too hungry for you the other night, sugar. This time we're going to take things slower."

He lowered his head and traced her lips with his tongue. When she opened for him, he slipped inside and reveled in the way she moaned and pressed herself to him. It was as if she were trying to become a part of him.

Trailing his hands down her neck to the slope of her breasts, then around to her sides, he gathered her pink T-shirt with his fingers. "Raise your arms for me, Cassie."

When she did as he commanded, he swept her shirt over her head, then made quick work of unfastening her bra. His hands shook slightly as he cupped her perfect breasts and chafed her taut nipples with his thumbs. As he watched, her eyes drifted shut and she grasped his arms for support.

"Feel good, sugar?" he asked, lowering his mouth to kiss the tight peaks.

Her lids fluttered open and the passion he saw in the depths of her emerald gaze made his body feel as if he'd been struck by a bolt of lightning. With one kiss, one touch, she wanted him just as much as he wanted her. He hoped like hell he could keep his promise to make things last.

When she unsnapped his shirt and pushed it from his shoulders, he reluctantly took his hands from her soft skin long enough to shrug out of the garment. But before he could return to the pleasurable task of loving her, she brought her hands up to his chest and ran her nails over his own puckered nipples, then trailed a finger down the line of hair that disappeared into his jeans. His soul caught fire.

"I lied," she said quietly.

So caught up in the sensation building a few inches below her finger, he didn't realize for a couple of seconds what she'd said. Her talented touch was playing hell with his concentration.

"What do you mean, you lied?" he asked through clenched teeth.

"The first day we met, I told you that your 'assets' weren't that memorable." She flashed her killer dimples at him. "It couldn't have been a bigger lie. The memory of your body has kept me awake nights."

Her admission sent his blood pressure skyrocketing. Taking a deep breath, he tried to slow down the pounding in his chest and the blood surging through his veins. "If you keep telling me things like that, you'll make me out a liar, too." At her questioning look, he chuckled. "I won't be able to take things slow."

"I'm not sure I want you to," Cassie said, unbuckling his belt.

She unsnapped his jeans, then, smiling, eased the zipper down over his pulsing erection. She trailed her fingertip along the hair from his navel to the waistband of his low-riding briefs, and he fought to maintain his control.

Shooing her hands away before he lost the last shred of his sanity, Logan made short work of sliding the rest of her clothing down her legs. When she stepped out of them, he took a deep breath. He'd never seen a more perfect woman in his entire thirty-four years.

"This isn't fair," she said, reaching for his waistband.

"I agree." Impatient to feel all of her against him, he shucked his jeans and briefs, then kicked them aside.

"You're beautiful," she said, her voice filled with awe.

Logan chuckled. "Women are beautiful. Men aren't."

She nodded. "You are."

He shook his head. "You're the one who's beautiful, perfect."

He pulled her to him and groaned as the feel of her skin warmed the depths of his soul. Desperate to convey everything he was feeling but couldn't voice, he kissed her until she shivered with desire.

Sliding his hand between them, he reached down to touch her intimately, and to his immense satisfaction she moaned and melted into him. "That's right, sugar. It's going to be much better this time because now I know exactly what makes you hot and ready for me. What makes you go crazy."

"But I have...the same advantage," she said, sounding breathless.

Her small hand found his erection and Logan

thought his head might fly right off his shoulders. Keeping his promise to take things more slowly was going to be next to impossible with her talented little hands holding him that way.

She stroked and caressed him with such tenderness, his chest tightened with emotion. He'd never have believed it, but his hunger for her was even stronger than before. He wanted her with every cell of his being, wanted to show her how much their lovemaking meant to him.

Not sure how much longer his legs would support him, he picked her up and carried her to his bed. Pushing back the covers, he placed her on the cool navy sheets, then quickly turned and walked into the half bath adjoining his room. When he returned, he stretched out beside her and tucked under his pillow the foil packet he'd retrieved from the medicine cabinet.

Gathering her to him, he enjoyed the feel of soft feminine skin against his heated body. There was so much he wanted to tell her, but all the romantic things women wanted to hear had never come easily to him. Instead of trying to put his feelings into words, Logan decided to love her slowly, thoroughly, and when it was over she'd have no doubt how much she meant to him, how much she'd become a part of him.

He kissed the hollow at the base of her throat, then nibbled his way to her breast. Teasing her nipples with his tongue, he felt his own excitement build when she moaned and tangled her fingers in his hair to hold him to her.

"Feel good?"

"Mmmm."

He smiled as he trailed kisses down her abdomen. "Hang on, sugar, it's going to get a lot better."

"Logan…no…" She sounded almost desperate.

He raised his head to meet her embarrassed gaze. "Do you trust me, Cassie?"

"Yes."

"Then lie back and let me give you pleasure."

She hesitated only a moment before lying back against the pillows. Her small body trembled and he realized they were breaking new ground for her. Apparently her husband had never taken the time to love every inch of her, to worship her with his lips as well as his body. The man had been a complete and utter fool.

Kissing her intimately, Logan was rewarded with her soft moans, the sight of her hands gripping the sheet beside her.

"Logan…please."

"What do you want, Cassie?" When she opened her eyes to look at him, he had no doubts what she wanted. But he needed to hear her tell him.

"Make love to me, Logan," she said, her words a throaty plea.

He slowly kissed his way back up her body. "But I wanted this to last awhile longer," he teased.

She opened her eyes and, holding his gaze, found him with her hands. His heart stalled, then took off at a dead run. Her silky palms slid along his shaft, stroking him, cupping his heaviness. Logan closed his eyes against the intense waves of need racing through him.

Taking her hands in his, he stopped her sensual

assault before he lost the last shred of his restraint. "Sugar, you've made your point."

When he reached for their protection, his frustration knew no bounds. He raised the pillow and searched for the foil packet. It wasn't there.

"Looking for this?" Cassie asked, holding it between her fingers. Relieved, he started to take it from her, but she shook her head. Opening the tiny package, she held his gaze as she rolled their protection over his fevered flesh.

The intense desire in her eyes, the feel of her hands on his body and the obvious fact that she was comfortable with the intimacy they shared had him throbbing with the need to make her his. "Sugar, I don't mean to rush things, but I can't stand much more of this."

Without a word she smiled, straddled his hips and, slowly easing herself down, took him inside. Logan had to grind his teeth and fight with every last ounce of strength he possessed to keep what small bit of sanity he had left.

Their gazes locked, Logan placed his hands on her hips to help her set a steady pace. He savored every moment of watching her expression change with the progression of her need. Her cheeks flushing with desire, her eyes sparkling with building passion and her willingness to share herself so intimately made his chest tighten. Cassie made love to him not only with her body, but with her heart and soul, as well.

He felt her tighten around him as she neared the peak, and his body bunched with the need to release himself inside her. Wanting, needing her to join him in the storm, Logan moved his hand to touch her intimately. Her body tightened instantly, and he felt her inner muscles quiver and clench around him as wave upon wave of sensation drew her into complete fulfillment.

The pull of Cassie's body, the undeniable ecstasy on her beautiful face triggered his own explosion, and, surging into her, Logan groaned from the soul-shattering pleasure draining his body.

Completely exhausted, Cassie collapsed on top of his chest. He wrapped his arms around her and held her close. She was incredible, and so responsive. He decided if he died at that very moment, he'd leave the world a happy, satisfied man.

It took him a moment to realize that what he was feeling ran far deeper than pleasure and desire. The emotion he'd had invading every cell in his being since he'd opened his eyes to find her perusing his body while he sat in the bathtub that first day just might be love.

Could he take the chance on loving Cassie, then have her leave the Lazy Ace because she couldn't stand the isolation? Or worse yet, what if she or one of the babies became ill and he couldn't get them to a doctor in time?

When Cassie had come down with the flu he'd been scared half out of his mind that she'd develop pneumonia, as his mother had. Could he survive something like that? Or would he be like his father? When Logan's mother died, Cal Murdock had allowed his pain to turn into hatred and had directed every ounce of it toward his only son.

Logan closed his eyes as deep longing and loneliness warred with years of pain and guilt. He didn't think he'd ever be that type of man, but he'd never loved anyone as completely as he loved Cassie and the girls.

And that scared the living hell out of him.

Ten

When Hank left the breakfast table, grabbed Ginny in a bear hug and kissed her, Logan wondered if the couple might not need oxygen before it was over. He glanced at Cassie. He'd like to do the same with her, but in private.

Winking at her, he grabbed his hat and tapped Hank on the shoulder. "Come on, old buddy." When Hank finally lifted his head, Logan chuckled. "If we don't get the cabin finished pretty soon, your first-born will be ready for college before the two of you get moved in."

"Hey, gimme a break," Hank said, grinning. "I'll finish the house after I finish makin' a baby."

"Well, now that you mention it..." Ginny beamed. "I passed the test just this morning. I'm pregnant."

"I'm gonna be a daddy!" Hank's shout of triumph could have been heard all the way down in Bear Creek.

Watching the happy couple embrace, Logan felt envy clench his gut. He glanced at Cassie. As ridiculous as the notion was, he found himself wishing they were the ones celebrating the good news of having a baby on the way.

In the three weeks following the camping trip, he and Cassie had shared as many nights together as they could without drawing attention to the fact that there was more between them than just joint ownership of the Lazy Ace. They'd talked about a lot of things during their nights together, but they hadn't verbally agreed to keep quiet about their...their what?

Affair?

No, that wasn't the right word. What he and Cassie shared ran much deeper than that.

Relationship?

He wasn't sure if that was the right word, either. Relationships screamed commitment and promises. But neither one of them had committed to anything, nor had they made any promises.

"Oh, Ginny, I'm so happy for you," Cassie said, leaving the table to hug her friend.

Logan slapped Hank on the shoulder. "Congratulations."

"Thanks," Hank said. Holding Ginny to his side, the man looked happier than Logan had ever seen him.

His gaze drifted back to Cassie. The idea of making a few promises didn't scare him as it would have a month ago.

He watched her move around the kitchen. She looked a lot like the way he felt—dazed and more than a little confused. He wondered if she was having similar thoughts.

"Logan?" Hank tapped him on the shoulder. "Are you gonna stand there all day, or are we workin' on the cabin?" Grinning at his wife, Hank added, "I have a nest to finish."

"Uh, sure," Logan said, jamming his Resistol on his head. His gaze lingered on Cassie for a moment longer, then he headed for the door.

He couldn't believe what was running through his mind, but making a commitment to Cassie and asking to become part of her little family was beginning to sound like a damned fine idea.

Her heart pounding in her chest like an out-of-control jackhammer, Cassie watched the men leave to work on the foreman's house. "Ginny, after we get the girls settled down to play, would you mind watching them for a few minutes?"

"No problem, Cass." Ginny wiped the babies' faces. "I'll play with them until they get sleepy, then I'll start making a list of things I want to pick up down in Laramie the next time we visit Hank's grandmother."

"Thanks," Cassie said, feeling as if the walls were closing in on her. She had to get upstairs and find her datebook.

"Are you all right, Cass? You look a little—" Ginny paused "—flustered? Upset?"

Cassie nodded as she handed Chelsea to Ginny, then turned back to pick up Kelsie. "I'm just a little tired, that's all."

Once they had the girls settled in the playpen, she barely resisted the urge to wring her hands as she waited for Ginny to come back downstairs with her notepad and pen. "I won't be long," Cassie said, surprised that she sounded calm, considering all the butterflies fluttering around in her stomach. "I have to check on a couple things."

"Take your time," Ginny said, smiling. "The girls and I will be just fine."

Cassie climbed the stairs on wobbly legs and barely managed to make it to her room before her nerves got the better of her. Tears blurred her eyes and her hands shook uncontrollably as she rummaged through her underwear drawer to find her personal calendar. She had to be mistaken about the dates.

Quickly checking the number of weeks since her last period, she bit her lower lip and moaned aloud. How could she be two weeks late?

She walked over and sank down on the bed. How on earth could this have happened? They'd always been so meticulous about protection. Not once had they...

The camping trip. They hadn't used anything that first night up in the mountains.

Reality slammed into her and had her frantically thumbing through the calendar once again. Adding up the days, she shook her head, then added them again just to be sure. This couldn't be happening. It was impossible.

But even as she stubbornly clung to the thought,

Cassie knew she was only fooling herself. It was not only possible, it was probable.

Just because their first night together should have been safe didn't mean it was. Countless babies had been conceived during a "safe time" of the month.

She closed her eyes and fought the panic clawing at her insides. How would she ever be able to tell Logan? How would he react?

Stan had insisted he wanted children until the day she found out the twins were on the way. But Logan had always made it clear that he wasn't father material and didn't want kids.

Feeling desperate, Cassie tried to think of other reasons for her missed period. Maybe she wasn't pregnant. Factors such as the flu or the excitement of moving to the ranch could have delayed her cycle. And the one sure sign that she was pregnant hadn't shown up.

Within days of conceiving the twins, she'd known beyond a shadow of doubt that she was expecting. It had been the only time in her life she'd ever experienced nausea. So far she hadn't even been queasy. Far from it. For the past few days she'd been eating like a horse and felt great.

Taking a deep breath, she rose to her feet and tucked the calendar back inside the drawer. She wouldn't think about it right now. She'd wait until the end of the week to see if she started. Only then would she allow herself to fall apart and have a full-fledged panic attack.

Two days later Cassie walked down the lane leading to the foreman's cabin, clutching the handle of the picnic basket. It had been Ginny's turn to take lunch to Logan and Hank, but suffering her first bout of morning sickness, she'd begged off and asked to play with the twins while Cassie went.

Cassie didn't mind the quarter-mile hike. It gave her the chance to enjoy the warm sun on her face and the crisp breeze that had already started changing the aspens from green to their early-autumn gold.

And it gave her time to think.

It had been two days since she'd realized that she might be pregnant with Logan's baby, and in that time she'd changed her mind at least a hundred times about what to do. She feared he might be like Stan and ask her to do something she'd never even consider. Or he could face up to his responsibility and offer financial help in supporting the child, but nothing more.

Cassie really didn't believe he'd take either stance on the matter. He'd seemed outraged when he'd learned about Stan's demands over her pregnancy with the twins, and she'd watched Logan with her daughters. He had too much love to give to turn his back on his own child.

But that posed another question. Why had he indicated that he never wanted children?

She shook her head. She didn't know. And the only logical conclusion she'd been able to come to in the past couple of days had been to tell Logan what she suspected about being pregnant, then proceed from there.

As she pondered how to break the news to him, the willows lining the small stream running parallel to the lane rustled. Cassie stopped and glanced around. Something wasn't right. The breeze had died and there was no reason for anything to be moving the branches, unless...there was something behind them? She swallowed hard.

Something big. Something very hairy. Something with a lot of teeth.

She started walking faster. Whatever was on the other side of the brush to her left was keeping up with her. Her heart beating double-time, she broke into a jog. The unidentified animal kept pace.

"Logan!" Over halfway to the little house, she hoped he could hear her. "Logan!"

Suddenly the bushes just ahead of her shook violently and she heard a loud grunt. Not more than a split second later a huge black bear emerged to block her path.

Cassie wasn't sure if it was Samson or another bear, but it didn't matter. She couldn't stop herself from screaming at the top of her lungs. But instead of the animal retreating as Samson had done up in the mountains, this bear just trained his beady bear eyes on her, sniffed the air, then opened his mouth and let loose with a loud bellow.

All she saw were a lot of large, yellow-white, sharp-looking teeth. She screamed again and closed her eyes. If he was going to devour her, she certainly didn't want to watch all of those teeth coming at her.

Just when she thought her heart would burst from pounding so hard, she heard a commotion and opened her eyes. Logan and Hank were running up behind the beast. Yelling and waving his arms, Logan diverted the bear's attention to himself and her heart stopped completely. What if the animal attacked him?

"Cassie, don't make a sound," Logan said, keeping his gaze on the bear. "Move slow and easy over toward Hank while I get Samson calmed down."

She glanced to her right. Hank stood several feet away, his face as white as a sheet of tissue paper. Doing as Logan had commanded, Cassie eased her way over to Hank. He immediately shoved her behind him, putting himself between her and possible danger.

Only then did she realize she still held the picnic basket. Food. Bear food. She released the death grip she had on the handle and, dropping it, peered around Hank to see if Logan was all right. To her amazement, the agitated bear stopped bellowing, sniffed the air, then stared at Logan.

"Hank, toss that picnic basket over here," Logan said, keeping several feet between himself and Samson.

Throwing the container to Logan, Hank walked over to a huge boulder and leaned against it. Cassie watched Logan catch the wicker basket, then toss it as far into the brush as he could. Samson stood for a moment sniffing the air before he grunted, then crashed through the brush in the direction the picnic basket had gone.

Hank took a deep breath. "My God, I think I just lost a good ten years off my life. I thought Ginny...I mean, she was supposed to—"

"Ginny got sick...after you left to come down here," Cassie said breathlessly. "She asked me to bring lunch to you and Logan."

Apparently satisfied that Samson was no longer a threat, Logan walked straight to Cassie and took her into his arms. "Are you all right?" At odds with his actions, he sounded angry.

Nodding, she burrowed into his embrace, not caring what Hank might think. "How often does he make an appearance around here?" she asked.

"Too often," Hank said disgustedly.

"I'm going to call Jim Bennett over at Fish and Wildlife and see if he can relocate Samson to one of the wilderness areas," Logan said, hugging her close. "Or maybe check around to see if there's a zoo in need of a bear."

"It's about damned time," Hank muttered. He pushed away from the boulder. "I'm going up to the house to check on Ginny. See you two later."

"You're shaking," Logan said, his tone gentle. "Come on. Let's get to the cabin and sit down."

Her legs felt as if rubber bands had replaced muscle, and Cassie had to lean on Logan in order to walk the rest of the way to the foreman's house. "I think from now on, I'll drive when I have to bring you and Hank lunch."

Logan shook his head. "From now on, we'll either take lunch with us or skip it." He lifted her to the opened tailgate of his truck, then sat down beside her and put his arm around her. "You sure you're okay?"

"I'll be fine." Leaning her head against his shoulder, she closed her eyes and took a deep breath to calm the uneasiness in the pit of her stomach. She could tell he was still angry by the rigid set of his jaw and the tension in his deep voice. Was he upset with her for screaming at his bear again?

"I'm sorry I screamed, but I don't think it scared Samson this time," she said. "I think he wanted your lunch."

"That's what bothers me," Logan said, his arm tightening around her. "He's losing all fear of humans."

They sat in silence for several minutes as Cassie drew strength from the man she loved with all her heart. She didn't know how to tell him she was almost certain he was going to be a father, or how he'd take the news. She wasn't even sure how to broach the subject.

Maybe if she started off by talking with him about the twins, then she could ask why he'd said he didn't want children. From there maybe she'd get a clue about how to proceed.

"Did you notice that Kelsie is getting another tooth?"

"So I'll be walking the floor with her again soon?" The anger in his voice had been replaced with tenderness at the mention of her daughter.

"I still don't know why you didn't wake me to take care of her."

"You were tired." He kissed the top of her head. "Besides, I didn't mind. Chelsea and Kelsie are cute kids."

"You're really good with children." She took a deep breath. He'd just given her the opening she'd been looking for. Now, if she could just find the courage to proceed. "Why did you tell me you weren't?"

Tension stiffened his body, but he remained silent.

Her stomach clenched. "Logan?"

"My father didn't set a very good example of the way a man should be around kids," he finally said, his voice tight. "I didn't want to make a child feel the way I did growing up."

She pulled from his arms to look at him. "What happened between you and your father?"

Closing his eyes, Logan shook his head. He didn't like talking about the past or the pain that remembering it always caused. But he supposed that if she and the twins were going to stay—and it was beginning to look as if they would—she might as well know what had happened.

"I was eleven when my mother died." He opened his eyes to stare off into the distance.

Cassie gasped. "Oh, Logan, I'm so sorry. I didn't realize you were so young when she died. What happened?"

"The west pasture didn't have good access to water, so during the summer my dad and I dammed up the stream and made a small watering hole." He took a deep breath. "That winter he assigned me the job of riding over there every day to chop a hole in the ice for the cattle to get water."

"That seems awfully young for that kind of chore," Cassie said gently.

"I'm sure that's what my mom thought, too," he said, nodding. "No matter how busy she was, or what she had left to do of her own chores, she always made sure she rode over there with me."

"She must have been a very good mother."

"She was." When he'd lost his mother, he'd lost

the only person in the world who'd loved him unconditionally. He had to clear his throat before he could continue. "Anyway, one day when we got there the pond was frozen over, like it always was. I was almost finished clearing a fairly good-sized hole when the ax flew out of my hands and slid out onto the ice. Mom said to leave it, but I knew Dad would raise hell about me losing a good ax, so I went out onto the ice after it."

"Oh, my God! You fell in."

Nodding, he closed his eyes against the pain knifing through him. "I slipped and went into the hole I'd just finished chopping. Mom didn't hesitate. She jumped off her horse and came in after me."

The tears running down Cassie's cheeks just about did him in. "Did your mother drown?"

"No. God only knows how, but she managed to drag us both out of the water and get us home." He swallowed around a lump the size of his fist, clogging his throat. "She got sick right after that, but didn't let on how bad she felt. By the time we realized how ill she was, a blizzard had moved through. It took three days before Dad could get her to the hospital down in Laramie. But it was too late. We lost her that night."

"I'm sure you and your father did all you could."

Logan's face hardened. "As far as my Dad was concerned, I'd done enough already."

"Your father blamed you?"

"Until the day he died," Logan said, nodding.

Her stomach knotted. "It wasn't your fault, Logan." How could a father blame his son for something the child couldn't prevent?

He nodded. "Reasoning tells me now that it wasn't." He thumped his chest. "But when I was a kid it felt like it was in here. If it weren't for Hank and his friendship, I wouldn't have had anyone."

Her stomach felt ready to revolt. How could a man lay that kind of senseless guilt on a child?

Everything began to make sense. No wonder Logan kept reminding her how far it was to town. It also explained why he'd hovered over her when she had the flu. He had been afraid she'd become as ill as his mother. And Cassie could well understand his fear of subjecting a child to the kind of treatment he'd received from his father.

She knew deep in her heart that Logan could never be like his father. But Logan didn't realize it yet, and she had no idea what to say to convince him or ease the years of pain he'd suffered.

The churning in her stomach increased, and she wasn't sure if it was due to the outrage she felt at his father's cruelty or from the baby nestled deep inside her. But she did know that if she didn't leave that very minute, she'd end up humiliating herself by being sick.

"Cassie, I've been meaning to ask you about something concerning Hank and the ranch," Logan said. "Would you have any objections to our giving him an interest in the Lazy Ace Cattle Company? He's been a loyal friend and—"

Her stomach lurched and she jumped to her feet. "I can't stay…any longer. I can't think…about it now. I have to leave."

Logan's chest tightened and his heart felt as if someone were trying to rip it from his body as he watched the only woman he'd ever loved run from him as if a pack of wolves nipped at her heels. She was leaving.

What had driven her away? Had she been repulsed by the sordid story of his mother's death? She'd said he wasn't to blame. Did she mean it? Or deep down did she think his father had been right?

Or could she have finally realized that although beautiful, this land was dangerous? Was she afraid that Samson would come back and one day threaten the girls?

Logan took a deep, shuddering breath, then another. Nothing eased the pain threatening to choke the life from him. His gaze scanned the mountains to the east, then the western horizon that seemed to go on forever. He'd just begun to believe she loved this rugged land as much as he did.

How could he have let himself fantasize that she wouldn't find the isolation intolerable? How could he have fooled himself into believing that he could always protect her and the babies from being harmed? Hell, he hadn't even been able to ensure her safety in the short quarter of a mile between the ranch house and the foreman's cabin.

Gazing at the log structure, he shook his head. Cassie and the babies would be leaving to go back to St. Louis and it would kill him if he had to watch them go. He'd get Hank to bring him some clothes and a few supplies. Then, after Cassie and the girls had cleared out, Hank and Ginny could have the ranch house and he'd move in down here.

He'd started the renovations on the cabin for Cassie and the twins to move in, thinking it would ensure his peace of mind. But Logan realized now that even if Hank hadn't decided to marry Ginny and claim the foreman's house, it would never have worked. Cassie had turned the ranch house into a home for all of them, and in doing so, she'd made it impossible for him to ever live there without her.

Eleven

Cassie looked up from the magazine she'd been thumbing through and glanced at the clock. Again. It was almost ten and Logan still hadn't returned from the cabin. When Hank had come home for dinner, all he'd said was Logan wouldn't be joining them. That had been over four hours ago. What could be taking him so long?

"Cass? Hank and I are going up to bed," Ginny said from the bottom of the stairs. All evening she and Hank had been sitting at the kitchen table, poring over baby-furniture catalogs and planning how they'd decorate their nursery. "How much longer are you going to stay up?"

"Oh, for a little while," Cassie said, feigning indifference. She needed to talk to Logan and she wasn't going to bed until she had.

Hank walked up behind Ginny and wrapped his arms around her waist. "Uh, Cassie, I think you might be up for quite some time if you're waiting on Logan. He's spending the night down at the foreman's house."

Shocked, Cassie tossed the magazine onto the couch beside her and jumped to her feet. "Why?"

"He said it would be easier to get started to work in the morning." The look on Hank's face told her he knew a lot more about the situation than he was telling.

"What's going on, Hank?" she demanded, not expecting much of an explanation.

"I can't say," Hank said, looking grim. "All I know is Logan said he'd be down there if anyone needed him." A slow grin replaced the man's troubled expression. "Do *you* know of anyone who needs him, Cassie?"

Hank hadn't exactly been a fountain of knowledge, but he was definitely trying to nudge her in the right direction. She looked to Ginny for a clue.

Her best friend smiled. "Cass, if you know of anyone who needs to make a trip down to the cabin tonight, tell them that Hank and I will be here in case the twins wake up."

"And while you're at it, you can tell whoever goes down there to let Logan know I've decided to take tomorrow morning off," Hank added.

Ginny nodded. "Hank and I are going to practice our baby skills. You wouldn't happen to know where we could find a couple of babies to take care of, would you?"

Tears filled Cassie's eyes as she rushed over to hug them both. "You two are the best. Thanks."

"You're not walking down there after what happened today with Samson, are you?" Ginny asked, concerned.

"No, I'll take my car."

Hank dug in his pocket, then handed Cassie a set of keys. "Your car is in the shed. Take my truck." He paused, his expression turning serious. "When you get down there, don't be surprised if Logan has the idea you might not be staying around much longer."

"He thinks we're leaving?" she asked incredulously. "What on earth gave him that idea?"

"Don't know," Hank said, shrugging. "But make him listen to reason."

"I will." Cassie grabbed her windbreaker from the hall closet and stuffed her arms into the sleeves. "Logan Murdock may be the most stubborn, aggravating soul I've ever met, but I know what I want."

"You go, girl!" Ginny said, laughing.

Cassie ran down the hall to the kitchen, then out the back door to Hank's truck. The man she loved was sitting a quarter of a mile away, thinking that she was leaving him. She had to set things straight.

As she inserted the key into the ignition, the thought that she might make a fool of herself crossed her mind, but she pushed it aside. Stan had rebelled at the thought of impending fatherhood. But he'd been selfish and immature. Logan was nothing like that. And she wouldn't allow her fears that he'd re-

ject her, the twins and the baby she carried to keep
her from trying to convince him they belonged together.

Sitting on the porch steps of the foreman's house,
Logan stared up at the stars. This afternoon had been
a prime example of what he'd tried to tell Cassie all
along. The Lazy Ace was no place for women and
kids. The weather was too harsh, and in the event of
an emergency the ranch was too remote. And just
today Samson had proved the dangers posed by the
natural predators of the area.

Of course, by calling his friend at Fish and Wildlife he'd already taken care of Samson and the threat
the bear posed. Samson would soon be on his way
to a closed area of a wilderness park in Montana
where contact with humans was a very remote pos-
sibility. He'd be away from human contact, and his
chances of survival would be much better now that
he'd apparently lost all fear of humans.

But Logan would be damned if he could figure out
how he was going to survive without Cassie. What
would the rest of his life be like?

Dismal was about the only word he could think of
that even came close to describing the hell he anticipated for the future.

If he thought it would make a difference in her
decision, he'd go crawling up to the house on his
hands and knees and beg her to stay. But he knew
she'd refuse. He might as well keep his pride. It was
about all he had left. She'd already taken his heart,
his soul.

The distant sound of a truck engine roaring to life
split the quiet night. Hank really needed to get that

muffler fixed. The damned thing was just plain offensive.

Logan could tell the vehicle was getting closer, and he wondered why his friend was driving down to the cabin. But it didn't matter. Hell, nothing mattered anymore. Cassie was leaving the Lazy Ace and that pretty much desensitized him to everything else.

God, he'd never realized a man could hurt so much or life could feel so hopeless. He took a deep, shuddering breath. It felt as if someone had reached inside him and ripped out his very soul, leaving him empty. Hollow.

He still didn't think he'd ever forgive his father for the hell he'd put him through, but Logan was beginning to understand what his father might have been feeling after his wife died. If Cal Murdock had loved Logan's mother as much as Logan loved Cassie, losing her had to have devastated the man.

When the truck pulled to a stop in front of the cabin, Logan took a deep breath and tried to adopt a benign expression. Hank didn't give up easily. Logan would give him that.

All afternoon Hank had practically talked himself blue, trying to get Logan to go up to the ranch house and straighten things out with Cassie. Logan had finally threatened to deck him before Hank shut up. And then he'd spent the rest of the afternoon muttering about boneheaded fools and stubborn jackasses. He'd probably come back to try one last time.

But Hank had promised to keep his mouth shut about the reason Logan was staying away from the ranch house. He had no doubt it would just about kill the man, but he knew Hank would do as he'd asked.

As the driver's door opened, Logan's heart stopped, then thumped so hard he thought it might crack a few ribs. Cassie was getting out of Hank's truck. What the hell was she doing down here? Why wasn't she up at the house? Had his misguided, meddling best friend betrayed him?

Or had something happened? Was something wrong with one of the babies?

"What are you doing down here, Logan?" she asked, walking toward him. "I've been waiting to talk to you all evening."

The sound of her soft voice and the sight of her slender figure silhouetted in the moonlight just about tore him apart. "I'm working."

She shook her head and sat down beside him. With her body so close to his, his hands shook from wanting to reach out to touch her.

"You can't work and sit on the steps gazing off into the night," she said gently. "What's wrong, Logan?"

He ignored her question. "What are you doing here, Cassie?"

He'd tried to keep his voice flat, but the strain of having her so close and not being able to hold her had added a harshness that made him wince. God, but he wanted to wrap his arms around her and never let go. He clenched his hands into tight balls to keep from doing just that.

"I can see you're back to your usual congenial self," she said dryly. "You really do need to work on your people skills, Logan."

He shrugged. "There's not a lot of need for people skills out here." His forearms rested on his knees;

he stared at his doubled fists. Every nerve in his body felt as if it twitched, and he rose to his feet to fight the restlessness. "You'd better go back to the house, Cassie. I've got an early day tomorrow and I'm going inside to get some sleep."

Jumping to her feet, she pushed on his chest and knocked him flat on his butt. "You're not going anywhere, buster. We've got things to talk over and you're going to listen to what I have to say."

The sudden anger in her voice confused him. What did she have to be angry about? She was the one making the decision to leave the ranch.

Logan closed his eyes, took a deep breath and rose to his feet again. "I think you pretty much said what was on your mind this afternoon."

"No, I didn't." To his surprise, she shoved him back down again with more force than he would have expected from a woman her size. She shook her finger in front of his nose. "If I have to tie you up, you're going to listen to what I have to say, Logan Murdock."

The lights from inside the cabin filtered out onto the front porch and illuminated her delicate features. Cassie was furious and absolutely gorgeous.

He sighed. He might as well let her have her say, let her get it out of her system and then live the rest of his life in misery, remembering how beautiful she'd been when she was spitting mad.

"What's on your mind, Cassie?"

She propped her hands on her shapely hips and stared down at him. "Just where did you get the idea that I'm going back to St. Louis?"

That answered his question about Hank's loyalty.

The next time he saw the man, Logan fully intended to knock the hell out of him.

"You told me—"

She glared at him. "I did no such thing."

"Yes, you did."

"*No,* I didn't."

He scrubbed his hands over his face. "Look, Cassie, this isn't getting us anywhere and I'm not up to bickering with you." When he finally looked up at her, it just about tore him apart to repeat what she'd said. "This afternoon you told me you had to get out of here and that you were leaving."

She stopped to look at him as if he might not be the brightest bulb in the lamp. "You thought I meant I'd be leaving the Lazy Ace?"

"What else was I to think? I'd just told you about my mother dying because of this place being to hell and gone from civilization."

Her expression softened and, kneeling in front of him, she took his hands in hers. "Logan, that was a freak accident. Maybe your mother would have lived if you'd been closer to town and maybe she wouldn't. We'll never know. But I promise you, you weren't to blame. You'd have gone in after her if the circumstances had been reversed, wouldn't you?"

He nodded.

She kissed his palms, and longing streaked straight through him. "Would it matter that much to you if I did leave the ranch?"

"Yes." The word was out before he could stop himself. But once he'd said it, he wasn't sorry. Life without her would be sheer hell, and there was no sense lying about it.

"Why, Logan? Why would it make a difference if the girls and I went back to St. Louis?"

Her gaze held him captive and it suddenly didn't matter anymore whether he had a shred of pride left. All he wanted was to be with Cassie and the twins— to be part of their family.

Reaching for her, he hauled her to his chest and buried his face in her red-gold hair. "Because I love you, Cassie. God knows I tried not to, but I love you with every fiber of my being."

She pulled back to look at him a moment before covering her face with her hands and bawling like a baby.

Now what was he supposed to do? He'd damned his pride, laid his heart on the line and told her he loved her—something he'd never said to any other woman—and it made her cry? Was the idea of his loving her that revolting?

Logan felt about as low as a man could possibly feel.

Then Cassie confused the hell out of him. She took her hands from her face, threw her arms around his neck and cried harder.

Lifting her to sit across his lap, he held her close and rocked back and forth. He had no idea what was going on, but she was in his arms again and he took that as a good sign.

When she managed to regain control of her runaway emotions, Cassie laughed and wiped her eyes. Logan looked as if he wasn't sure whether to smile back or run for cover.

"You okay?" he asked, sounding cautious.

Cassie nodded. "I'm sorry. It's just…I mean, my

emotions are so…'' She paused, trying to think of a way to ease into the announcement that could very well destroy their relationship. ''Hormones,'' she finally said.

''Oh.'' His expression changed to one of understanding, and he nodded. ''I was wondering when that would happen.'' He pulled her back against his chest and hugged her close. ''So you're not leaving the ranch?''

''Absolutely not. Wild horses couldn't drag me away. I love it here.''

He was silent for several minutes, then she felt his chest rise as he took a deep breath. ''Why did you tell me you were leaving?''

''I didn't want to embarrass myself by being sick in front of you,'' she said, knowing that in the next few minutes there would be no turning back.

''I'm sorry, sugar,'' he said, his large hand gently rubbing her back. ''I didn't realize that Samson had scared you that badly.''

''He didn't.'' She took a deep breath, then another. Leaning back, she met his questioning gaze. ''Yes, I was very frightened, but there's another reason for my nausea.''

''Are you sick?'' he demanded, looking extremely worried.

''Not really.''

She bit her lower lip and closed her eyes. She'd never felt more unsure, but Logan had a right to know. She'd make her announcement and know exactly what his reaction would be to the news that sent some men running for their lives.

''Cassie?'' Logan cupped her cheek with his hand

and she found herself leaning into his touch, reveling in the feel of his tender caress.

Opening her eyes, she met his concerned gaze. "I love you with all my heart."

He smiled. "And I love you."

The more she thought about it, the more it made sense. She and the twins were a package deal. And she needed to know if he loved her enough to take on that kind of responsibility.

"Logan, will you marry me?"

"You'd better believe I will, sugar." She was sure they heard his happy exclamation all the way to Bear Creek. Hugging her, he laughed. "I was just trying to screw up my courage to ask you."

He kissed her then with such tenderness, Cassie felt as if she might faint. Love and a passion that transcended the physical left her breathless, and when he finally broke the kiss she felt the hard evidence of his desire against her hip. She wanted to show him how much she loved him, but they had one more issue to settle.

She sighed. Now came the most difficult part of all. Would he change his mind once she told him about the baby? Would he ask her to make a choice, as Stan had? Or would he be happy to learn he was going to be a father?

Before she had a chance to decide how to phrase things, he asked, "Sugar, would you mind if I adopt Chelsea and Kelsie once we get married?"

Tears pooled in her eyes and a lump clogged her throat. "Oh, Logan, the girls absolutely adore you."

"I love them, too." He beamed. "I already feel like they're my kids."

That did it. The floodgates opened and the tears rolled down her cheeks to drip off her chin.

Every time Cassie cried, Logan felt as if something was trying to squeeze his heart in two. "Don't cry, sugar." He pulled her back to his chest and held her close. She hadn't answered whether she wanted him to be the girls' daddy or not. "Are you crying happy tears?" he asked, hoping like hell that was the case.

She nodded.

"Then my wanting to adopt the twins makes you happy?"

Nodding again, she cried harder. He felt a little better, but this monthly hormone stuff was going to take some getting used to.

When she finally stopped crying again, he reached into his hip pocket and withdrew his bandanna. Wiping her eyes and nose, he smiled. "I take it you're going to allow me to be the twins' daddy?"

Her emerald eyes sparkled and she took his hand in hers. Placing it on her stomach, she said, "Yes. I want the girls to have the same last name as this baby."

The air rushed from Logan's lungs in a huge whoosh. He suddenly felt as if the world had come to a complete standstill. "Baby?" His voice cracked and he had to clear his throat. "You're pregnant?"

She nodded and bit her lower lip a moment before she cautiously said, "I'm going to have your baby, Logan."

He could tell she feared he'd have a reaction similar to her late husband's when he'd learned he was to be a father. She had nothing to worry about. Cassie had just handed him every one of his forbidden dreams on a silver platter.

"Sugar, you've made me the happiest man in the whole damned state," he said, cupping her face with his hands. "I've just gone from having nothing to having everything I've always wanted."

Cassie threw her arms around his shoulders, kissed him soundly, then grinned. "There's something else."

He grinned right back. "What's that, sugar?"

"I like the idea of you giving Hank an interest in the Lazy Ace."

Logan chuckled. "I wasn't sure you remembered that."

Smiling, she nodded. "I was just trying so hard not to be sick, I didn't have time to answer."

"Would you like to move into town so you can be close to a doctor?" he asked. He'd hate it, but it might be best for her, the twins and the new baby.

"Why on earth would we move to town when we live in the most beautiful place on earth?" she asked, frowning.

"I just thought—"

"No." She grinned. "I've told you before and it looks like I'll have to tell you again. The Lazy Ace is home. It's where we'll live, raise our children and grow old together."

He lowered his lips to kiss her. Cassie had barged into his life and given him everything he'd ever wanted, but never hoped to have.

And he couldn't have been happier about her invasion.

Epilogue

"Logan?"

His eyes still closed, Logan sleepily rolled over in bed to drape his arm over Cassie's rounded belly. He nuzzled the back of her neck. "What, sugar?"

"It's time," she said, her soft voice sounding a little strained.

"Time for what?"

"Time to go."

Instantly awake, Logan jumped out of bed to stare down at his extremely pregnant wife. "You mean it's *time?*"

Cassie laughed. "Yes, darling. I just had my first contraction."

"But you're only eight months, one week and two days along," he said, yanking a pair of jeans from the closet.

How could Cassie be so calm? From the time the obstetrician in Laramie had pinpointed her due date, he had kept track of how close the big event was, figured out the best route to take to the hospital and estimated how long it would take to get her there.

"Darling, the doctor and I have both told you that twins usually arrive early. I was only seven months and three weeks along when the girls were born." She grinned and reached for his hand to pull herself to a sitting position on the side of the bed. "Don't worry so much. There's plenty of time. It was a very mild contraction and if I hadn't promised I'd let you know the minute they started, you'd still be sleeping."

"For God's sake, woman, how can you be so calm?" he asked, stuffing his arms into his shirtsleeves. "You're having twins and the hospital is a hundred miles away."

"I've had twins before, remember?" she said, laughing.

"I haven't." He pulled on his socks and boots. "Now, get ready to go while I call the cabin and have Hank and Ginny come up here to stay with Chelsea and Kelsie."

Three days later Logan stood in the newly decorated nursery, holding his daughters as he introduced them to their new baby brothers. "The one getting his diaper changed is Kevin and the one in the bassinet is Kyle."

"Logan, darling, you've got them switched again," Cassie said, laughing. "I'm changing Kyle. Kevin will get his diaper changed next."

Pride and happiness filled his heart as he grinned at his beautiful wife. Cassie was the most amazing woman he'd ever known. She'd put up with eight months of his hovering over her like a worried mother hen, endured a record-breaking ride to the hospital down in Laramie and not only delivered healthy identical twin boys, she could already tell them apart.

"I will get better at this. Right?"

Cassie smiled. "You learned to tell Kelsie and Chelsea apart, didn't you?"

Logan kissed each one of his daughters, then set them down on the floor to play. Walking over to the bassinet, he lifted Kevin to carry him over to Cassie for a diaper change. She handed Kyle to him and Logan cradled the baby to his chest.

"I had to be around the girls awhile, but it didn't take long," he said, holding his finger to his son's little hand.

The dark-haired infant wrapped his tiny fingers around Logan's and squeezed. He was filled with such pride, he thought he just might pop the snaps open on his chambray shirt. The kid was damned strong for only being three days old.

He watched Cassie finish diapering Kevin, then place the sleepy baby in one of the tiny beds. She indicated for him to put Kyle in the other. Holding her finger to her lips, she ushered everyone out into the hall.

He put his arm around Cassie's shoulders as they watched their daughters toddle off toward their room, more interested in playing with their toys than their new brothers. "Why don't you lie down for a while, sugar? I'll get the girls down for a nap."

Yawning, Cassie gazed up at him. "Thanks. I am a little tired."

He walked her to their room, wishing he could join her in bed, but knowing it would be several weeks before they'd be able to make love again. It was going to be sheer torture not being able to show her how much he loved her.

At the door she turned back. "Have you heard anything from Hank yet?"

Logan nodded. "He called about an hour ago to say Ginny was in the second stage of labor. Good thing the sonogram indicated they were having the boy they both wanted."

"Why?"

He chuckled. "This may be the only baby they have. Ginny's already threatened Hank with castration if he ever gets her pregnant again."

Cassie laughed. "She'll get over that. How's *he* doing?"

"Not real well. He made fun of me driving like a bat out of hell to get you to the hospital, but he beat my record by ten minutes." Logan grinned. "And they've already used smelling salts on him twice."

Logan felt two sets of tiny arms wrap around his knees. When he looked down, Chelsea and Kelsie gazed up and grinned at him. He grinned back. Apparently they'd already lost interest in playing.

Reaching down, he picked up both of his daughters. "Kiss Mommy and we'll let her get some rest before your brothers wake up." When the twins finished planting wet baby kisses on Cassie's cheeks, he set them on their feet. "Go crawl in bed, and Daddy will be there in just a minute to tuck you in."

He gave Cassie a quick kiss, then, after glancing into the nursery at his sons, he started down the hall toward his daughters' room. His chest tightened with emotion and more love than he'd ever dreamed possible.

His life was finally perfect and complete. He was married to the most exciting woman imaginable, he had two beautiful daughters and two healthy newborn sons. And when he and Cassie had given Hank a third interest in the ranch, Logan had realized his plans of going into business with his best friend.

At the girls' door he turned back to look at Cassie. She'd invaded his home, his heart and his soul.

She flashed her killer dimples at him. "I love you, Logan."

"And I love you, sugar," he said, feeling like the luckiest man alive.

* * * * *

Be sure to catch Kathie DeNosky's
next Desire novel, coming in August 2002.

Silhouette Desire

presents

DYNASTIES:
THE
CONNELLYS

A brand-new miniseries about the Connellys of Chicago,
a wealthy, powerful American family tied by blood to the
royal family of the island kingdom of Altaria.
They're wealthy, powerful and rocked by
scandal, betrayal…and passion!

Look for a whole year of glamorous and
utterly romantic tales in 2002:

Silhouette®
Where love comes alive™

Visit Silhouette at www.eHarlequin.com   SDDYN02

ANN MAJOR
CHRISTINE RIMMER
BEVERLY BARTON

cordially invite you to attend the year's most exclusive party at the **LONE STAR COUNTRY CLUB!**

Meet three very different young women who'll discover that wishes *can* come true!

LONE STAR
COUNTRY CLUB:
The Debutantes

Lone Star Country Club:
Where Texas society reigns
supreme—and appearances
are *everything*.

Available in May
at your favorite retail outlet,
only from Silhouette.

Silhouette®
Where love comes alive™

If you enjoyed what you just read,
then we've got an offer you can't resist!

Take 2 bestselling
love stories FREE!

Plus get a FREE surprise gift!

You are invited to enter the exclusive, masculine world of the...

Silhouette Desire's powerful miniseries features five wealthy Texas bachelors—all members of the state's most prestigious club—who set out to uncover a traitor in their midst... and discover their true loves!

THE MILLIONAIRE'S PREGNANT BRIDE
by Dixie Browning
February 2002 (SD #1420)

HER LONE STAR PROTECTOR
by Peggy Moreland
March 2002 (SD #1426)

TALL, DARK...AND FRAMED?
by Cathleen Galitz
April 2002 (SD #1433)

THE PLAYBOY MEETS HIS MATCH
by Sara Orwig
May 2002 (SD #1438)

THE BACHELOR TAKES A WIFE
by Jackie Merritt
June 2002 (SD #1444)

Available at your favorite retail outlet.